Bear's Heart

Corie J. Weaver

TITLES BY CORIE J. WEAVER

Mirror of Stone

New Legends of the Southwest
Coyote's Daughter
Bear's Heart

CHAPTER ONE

TIME MOVED IN A DANCE of days and then the long sleep of winter arrived. My family does not have to sleep through the winter and in truth, we do not. I leave the cave of our home to watch the snow fly across the land at least once or twice most years. But even with a bear's coat, winter is best spent curled up and dreaming of friends.

I woke slowly this year, tangled and trapped in the last of my dreams. They sang in my head, awkward and uncomfortable. Before I opened my eyes I stretched and twisted, then straightened my legs. A long sleep, even on a well-padded pallet, always leaves me a bit stiff despite my youth. I breathed deeply and the faint tang of smoke coiled onto my tongue. Mother and Father must already be up, I thought.

I stood, shook myself and padded about the cave. That they had allowed me to sleep in until the afternoon surprised me, an unusual treat. In the months before the sleep, they had taken my training more seriously than before. The question of my future had never been in doubt. I would be a healer, as they were, as all in my family had been.

The summer before had brought changes to our world and the casual teachings of previous years had been replaced with a landslide of information. Change comes infrequently to our land and I think what happened that year frightened them a little.

It is odd to think of my parents frightened of anything. When I was very young, I wondered if my father was slower of mind than other people. He is not fast with words or easy in conversation. Only as I grew did I realize he speaks nothing without weighing both his words and the reaction of his listener.

My mother is the sun to his moon. Her hands fly like quick bird wings and her speech runs fast and cheerful. She is delicate of feature, but I have seen her hold down patients as they thrash in fever. Through it all she never loses her poise.

For all my life I have trained to be a healer, a doctor, like them, but I hold a secret tight to my heart: fear. Fear that I will never truly be able to be like them, never possess the solid kindness of my father, the strength and grace of my mother. Never know always what to do, what to say.

And if I failed, people would die. For that is the burden of a healer.

No. I stopped these bleak thoughts; I would not let my fears burst forth, not on this first day after winter when new leaves would emerge.

In a corner of the cave we had designated for storage I reached above my head to check the contents of the dark red-and-tan woven basket. In the spring, there were always many patients with aches and pains and the pith of yucca bark makes a strong tea to help those afflicted with joint stiffness. Besides, the plant is good for washing and I looked forward to a long soak and thorough scrub.

Then I blinked in surprise. Before me, a heavy paw covered in honey-gold fur and tipped with long, curved nails, reached for the woven lid.

I sighed. I must still not be quite awake, to forget which shape I wore. I lowered my paw and began the shift in my mind.

I know well how the change appears to others; I have watched my parents shift from one shape to the other.

A bear, black and towering, or golden and sleek, stands before you, pauses, then reaches his paws towards the sky, as if to pull down the sun. Then with a movement swift as a hawk, the paws pass in front of the face, down the center of the body and spread to the side. No slower than that, you are faced with a man or woman who wears an elaborate bearskin coat, which can be removed and hung on a peg, like any coat.

It looks so simple. However, the shift is anything but. As a child I would spend days in bear form, forgetting how to shift into a girl, unable to hold the girl shape in my thoughts and uncomprehending of why I should bother. I have to hold the image clearly in my mind. If I fail, nothing bad happens, I simply do not change. And there is nothing wrong with staying a bear. But a bear's paw is ill-suited for some tasks. Many days, I find it is convenient to have the option of fingers.

I stood, quieted my mind and thought about being a girl, wrapped myself in that shape, as comfortable as my fur. As my hands flew down my body, the familiar crackling sensation came, like lightning striking. No pain, not exactly, but a tingle that began at the center of my chest and wrapped over my skin. I wondered, as I often do, if this is how snakes feel as they shed from one skin to the next.

I pushed the hood of my coat back and wrinkled my nose as I ran my fingers through waist-long black hair. Yes; definitely time for a bath. I checked the basket, relieved to find the contents full to the lip. I had spent the fall gathering supplies to hang and dry and did not want to spend my first day awake scouting for more plants.

I filled the clay pot with water from the trickling spring at the back of the cave and shivered at its chill, then placed the pot next to the banked fire to warm and pulled my fur coat around me tightly. Time to go outside, at least to gather a bit more wood. My parents' rule is to replace supplies as soon as they are used, preferably beforehand, so we are never caught short, never run out. In an emergency, such a shortage could mean disaster. I know their rules make sense, but sometimes I wish I did not have to bother, could wait until later.

As I walked to the front of the cave, I frowned. That both of my parents had been gone for so long was more than passing odd to me. Usually we spend the first day together, talking over plans for the new season, checking over our home for any repairs that might have become necessary since fall crept into winter.

Still, I was not worried. At sixteen summers, I often felt they fretted over me, kept me closer than needed. Perhaps this was the beginning of the year when they would allow me more freedom, a chance to be on my own. Maybe... I stopped, my hand on the door to the cave. Maybe this year I could bring up the question of when I would be permitted to move into my own quarters. I grinned and opened the seal to the door in the cliff.

And the smile froze on my face. Flurries of snow drifted across my vision. Unusual, but not unheard of. Weather here is unpredictable. Snow will fall in early summer some years, not at all in others. The wind was what stopped me in my tracks.

Cold, biting, the wind moaned across the desert. The sound cut me, the howls sobbed, tore at my heart. I fell to my knees at the door and stared at the desert. The dusting of snow lent the land a ghostly aspect. As I knelt, words repeated in my mind, a loop, frozen in place.

The land is dying.

My parents found me collapsed by the still open door to the cliff. They must have approached from around the side of the cliff even as I came outside, for I do not think I sat long on the ground.

My father scooped me up into his arms, his fur tickling my face.

He placed me by the fire and my mother stepped out of her coat with swift movements and placed her hands on my forehead.

"Bear Girl, what were you thinking?" She gazed at me, her dark-brown eyes wide, still checking me for harm.

"Mother, I am fine, truly." I stilled her hands with mine as they fluttered over me. "I do not know why I fell. I went out to get more firewood and," I stopped, remembering, "the wind. The sound of the wind..." My voice faded, unable to explain what I felt.

I needed no further explanation. My parents looked at each other and my mother's lips pressed into a thin line. My father nodded and my mother turned back to me.

"The wind has blown for days now. Our family did not hear the cry inside our home, the walls are too thick. But when your father and I left this morning, the sound shook us. We have spent the day checking on those who live near us. Many have been stricken by the wind with despair, fever and listlessness. Your father and I do not know what sickness this strange wind brings, but the illness is all around us now."

My father put his paw on my shoulder. "The sight of you lying motionless by the door, after we had seen so many ill, frightened us." His grip tightened. "Until the wind stops, perhaps you should stay inside."

I tilted my head to rest my cheek on his paw. "It frightened me, too." I straightened and looked up at him. "I think I was overcome by the strangeness, the suddenness. If I am expecting the wind, I do not believe I will fall again. If I am to be a healer, then I can not stay inside and hide."

My mother bowed her head at my words and the dark wings of her hair curtained her face. "Let us speak more of this later. Your father and I are tired past imagining. This is not a favorable start to a new year." She rose and walked towards her sleeping mat.

My father followed her. "Daughter, would you begin to prepare dinner? We can talk more after we rest and eat."

I stared after them. Whatever they had found outside must have been more terrible than I could imagine, for them to be so affected.

In baskets that rested on stone ledges I found dried venison and wrinkled red berries. Baskets of ground cornmeal dangled from leather cords, part of father's ongoing battle to keep the mice out of our pantry. After I nestled a clay pot in the ashes of the fire with the meat soaking within, I stirred water into the cornmeal and spread the mixture on a large, flat rock. A simple meal, but easy to prepare with what we had on hand. As I waited for the cakes to brown, I gazed into the fire and thought about the strange sobbing wind.

The flames sparkled, gold and red and orange in turn, reaching towards the smoke-hole drilled into the ceiling far above. I watched their dance, felt myself drawn in, my vision blurred by their flickering movement.

A girl sat in an enclosed courtyard and looked out through the gates as she sat carding baskets of wool under the spreading shade of a cottonwood tree. In the fields outside a ragged group of men and women searched for any ears of corn they could find, no matter how scrawny.

The appearance of a dark-haired young man trotting through the gates brought a deep flush to her cheeks.

"Tomás!"

He flashed a brilliant smile and detoured towards her, covering the ground between them with long, easy strides.

The girl put the carding combs into the basket of uncarded wool and hastily brushed loose tufts of wool from her long embroidered skirts and pulled her braids to lay straight down the front of her blouse.

"Is there anything wrong?"

He shook his head. "No, Isabel, nothing for you to worry about. A while back, the Brother asked the headman to keep an eye on the northern road for him. Some of our people have seen what looks to be a company of Otermín's men headed this way."

Isabel frowned. "I wonder why?"

Tomás no longer smiled. "The old men talk, but..." He trailed off and glanced around. "Now is not the time. Let me deliver my message to the Brother."

He stepped towards her, eyes bright. "But, first, a reward for the messenger." He bent towards her and stole a kiss, too quickly for her to duck away.

She pushed him back, laughing. "Stop it! You know you still must talk to my father."

He heaved a great sigh, but still grinned. She reached forward to toss his braid back over his bare shoulder. "He will be back any day now. The caravan completes the circuit from New Spain every three years; it will pass through Santa Catalina on the way north to Santa Fe."

"The caravan is late, the soldiers say." Tómas scowled.

"Then it's sure to arrive soon now, be patient," Isabel answered. Her tone sounded light, but her lips pressed together in a tight line.

Tomás threw his hands over his head. "You have said that for a month now. Ah, nevermind, everything will work out." He brushed her cheek with his hand, cupped her face so she looked directly into his eyes. "But now I must deliver my message. It would be bad if the governor"s men arrive before me."

She smiled and followed him with her eyes as he entered the cool shade of the building behind her.

A soft caress against her ankles made her jump. She looked down to discover the fluffy tail of a large black-and-white cat swishing back and forth from the basket of wool at her feet.

"Nicco, get out of there!"

Golden eyes framed in a black mask peered up at her over a perfect pink triangle of nose. He yawned, showing off his sharp white teeth and the ridges going down the matching pink roof of his mouth.

Isabel sighed and carefully detangled the cat from the basket of wool. Task completed, she sat back down on the rough wooden bench, the cat sprawled across her lap. She looked out of the courtyard towards the fields. The heat shimmered like flames before her eyes.

The smell of lightly scorched cakes startled me. I flipped them over quickly, burning my fingers, while I wondered what had just happened. A dream? The images of the girl, Isabel, the strange place, all were so clear. They did not have the feel of a dream, rather a memory. A memory I could not possibly have. I puzzled over the images and sucked my scorched fingers. My parents returned from the section of the cave where their sleeping chamber lay and the shadows in their eyes made me resolve to worry about my own insignificant problems later.

CHAPTER TWO

THE FIRST WEEK OF THE strange spring grew harder on my mother and father. Their rounds took longer as the sickness of the crying wind struck more victims. At night, they ate listlessly, barely able to stay awake before returning to their beds.

"We've tried chía leaves and they calm the fever, but do nothing to relieve the restlessness. Bark of the cottonwood tree serves no purpose, even though in the past it has worked in similar cases."

Father shook his head. "There are no cases like this."

They poured over their knowledge, racked their memories for obscure cures, concocted doses of medicines they had only heard of and had never, until now, had reason to use.

To no avail. The strange sickness gripped our valley and the sobbing wind continued, wearing down the hopes and spirits of all who lived within.

I stirred the stew. "Father, you are running low on too many things. You must let me go collect what plants are available."

He shook his head. "No. I do not want you exposed to the wind any more than necessary. It drains the strength and we have already seen you have little resistance to it."

I rolled my eyes. We had circled around this point every evening. They could not tend their patients, gather herbs and tend to the errands needed to keep our house. They had been trying to do it all themselves, but the effort exhausted them.

"Father, the wind surprised me that day. I know of it now; I will not succumb again. I am stronger than that."

Mother raised her head. "She is right, you know."

Father turned to her, surprise clear on his face.

"We need help," she said. "And someday we will not be here to advise her. Besides, my husband, she is your child. I would be surprised if she did not have your strength, as well."

The next morning I went to the door of the cave for the first time since my father had carried me in. They stood behind me, watching.

"Perhaps your bear form would be best."

I sighed. "Father, let us first see how this goes."

I opened the cliff side and stepped out.

The wind whistled around me, hideous in its power. I could feel the gusts pull at me, tug my energy away. I bit my lower lip and took another step outside. This could not defeat me. My step faltered and I heard my father shift behind me, then the whispered words of my mother.

"Wait. Watch. She can do this, she is strong."

I took another step as an answer to her faith.

The longer I was outside, the more the wind pressed, pulled, the more it sought to invade. But the longer I stood in it, the more I felt I understood it, did not fear it.

I walked, conscious of my back straightening, and then turned to face them in the doorway.

They stood holding hands and the pride fought with worry on their faces.

"Now will you let me help?"

Two days later I almost regretted having made a stand. I had scoured the nearby area for herbs and now needed to widen my search pattern, going further and further from home so that I did not overharvest any particular area.

The strange wind continued. No one had died of its effects yet, but my parents were certain it was only a matter of time before the oldest and weakest of their patients succumbed.

I brought an armload of wood into the cave, sealed the door behind me and leaned against the wall, shaking. Even if my parents could find a cure for the sickness of the wind, we were powerless to stop it from returning. No one, not even those who did not sleep through winter, had an explanation for what happened. It had begun with no warning, and from the first, those who heard it felt loss and sorrow in its song. The strength of the wind only grew with time.

Something had to be done.

It was clear to me the wind was magical, unnatural; therefore, defeating the wind would be outside of the reach of my family's abilities. Yes, members of my family can change our shape, but that is the limit of our magic, our pinang. We are not sorcerers. That is not our family's path.

I paused while stacking the wood. But we know someone who does walk that path, I thought, with a trill of nerves.

By the time my parents returned for the evening meal I had my arguments prepared. Looking at their exhausted faces I hesitated, reluctant to proceed with my plan. Building a trap, even for their own good, while they were so defenseless was unfair. Then my father stumbled, caught himself on a wall. He forced himself to stand straight and moved on, but I shook. If my father could be so weakened, then I had to do something. I swallowed, tongue thick in my mouth. I had decided upon the best way—the only way—and they must now be made to see it.

I served them warm, fresh cakes of bread smeared with a thin sheen of honey and dotted with glistening deep-red berries. The sweet wouldn't make them agree more easily, but it might put them in a better mood. Besides, by the way their shoulders slumped, I could tell they badly needed the extra energy the sugar would provide.

"I found more osha today."

My father looked up. "You did not take all of it, did you?"

"Of course, I did. I dug up every root I could see, so that there would be nothing to spread back next year when we need it again." I grinned at him. "I do remember some things you've taught me. I only took a portion and made sure to remember where the growth was so we can revisit that patch later."

Osha is good for many things, cures most winter sickness, helps with the racking coughs and bound up lungs and sore throats. So far it had not shown to be a help to us now, but my parents still held hope. They had to. Hope was all we had left.

"Do any of your patients sleep better today?"

Mother shrugged one shoulder. "Not that we can tell. Most say they can only hear the wind, hear voices crying and spend their nights trying to understand the words. Blue Snake Woman says to all who can still hear that the voice is that of her daughter who died in the river flood so many years ago."

My ears pricked at this. So maybe there was an answer after all? Maybe this was a ghost that could be put to rest?

My father continued. "But Spotted Feather Man swears it is his wife that he buried last summer. Says he hears her voice telling him how to find her, to bring her back."

I shuddered. From time to time parents and spouses did manage to bring back their loved ones from death, but no matter how much they tried, no matter how much they had loved each other, the return never worked out the way they hoped and became more of a heartbreak than the original death.

"Everyone we've spoken to hears a different voice on the wind, always someone they've lost, but they can't make out the words. I fear..." and he trailed off.

This would be my chance.

"Clearly, this is nothing natural. This is not just the usual winter wind, bringing coughs and aches. Father, Mother, this is sorcery and on our own we cannot defeat it. You must know this."

Father stared at me as if I had struck my head and wandered in my wits. "Of course we know this. Cub, we may be old, but we are not stupid."

I sat back. If they knew, then why hadn't they done anything?

"But, then..."

"Why have we not gone for help?" My mother gazed into the fire. "We have all we can manage to care for the people of our valley. This is our charge, our responsibility. This takes both of us, every moment, every bit of our energy. If one were to leave, the other would be unable to carry on."

She looked at me and shook her head, her hair swung like a sheet of dark rain behind her. "Your father and I have discussed this, many times. We cannot leave now, and there are none left who could make the journey, only children. We must wait."

I struck the ground with the flat of my hand. "Then send me! I will make sure you have sufficient supplies in the larder, that you have firewood for while I am gone, that all the baskets are full so you run out of nothing. I've made the trip before; I would be back in two days."

My father set his jaw. "No. I will not have it. I know you have gone there before, but never truly on your own. And for you to be outside and traveling through the wind for a full day each way would only ensure you fell sick, like the others. You have been more resilient to the wind than most, but I will not risk this."

I turned to appeal to my mother, but she only pressed her lips together and closed her eyes tight. "No. I agree with your father. It is not your duty yet. He and I will determine a way to get help if we can, but you are not old enough to make the journey." She rubbed her forehead and swallowed. She opened her soft, pleading eyes and crossed her arms over her chest. Her long thin hands grasped her shoulders so tightly her knuckles streaked white. "I would not hear your voice on the wind, daughter. I cannot stand the thought."

I spoke no more on the matter, knowing it grieved them, but late that night I lay on my bed and planned.

In the morning after they left, I straightened the cave around me, cleaned the clay pots from our early meal, checked the levels of the supplies in the back, and banked the fire. All was well. I had overstocked the larder, to the point of having several weeks laid in of most of our staples. The woodpile came to my shoulders and stretched across the wall twice the reach of my arms.

This time I would carry no gifts, despite tradition. I would not risk taking anything my parents might need in my absence. I ignored the quiet voice that reminded me what they would want most would be my presence, to be reassured I did not lie unconscious, or worse, on the ground, somewhere out of reach, somewhere they might never find my body.

I walked to the door, put my hand on the seal and stopped. I had never disobeyed my parents before in such a matter. Argued, fought with them, of course. Stretched the rules occasionally, perhaps. But never deliberately gone out of my way to do something they had forbidden.

I knew why they worried, of course. Years before I was born, there had been another child, a boy. And he had grown straight and tall and ran and played in the woods around our cave. And one bright summer day, while my family enjoyed the warmth of the sun, my brother had gone chasing after butterflies, or a bright colored bird. Something. They never knew, only that he had disappeared, had wandered outside of the allowed area. They searched, our friends and neighbors searched, for two days, all through the nights.

Until finally his small body was found trapped in the roots of a tree that grew on a bend of the bank of the river.

My parents never forgot him, made sure that I knew I had a brother, even if I would never meet him. Sometimes when my mother's eyes looked into the forest, I knew she was still waiting for her son, wondering what she had done wrong to let this happen.

But that happened many years ago and my brother was a child when the accident happened. I was nearly grown and this was a different situation, one that required action. I did not want my mother to hear my own voice on the wind.

I opened the door and stepped into the wind. Closing the door behind me, I ran my hand over it, to make sure it closed completely, with no crack to let the wind in. Only a solid cliff now stood before me.

No more delays. I put the hood of my coat up and pulled it low over my forehead. I called my image of the bear to mind, soft and golden, large and swift and drew the power into my hands. I bent down, touched the earth, the source of our power, then straightened, pulling the power up and over me in a towering wash. For a brief moment my vision filled with gold sparks, as if I had fallen into the sun.

The change complete, I lowered myself to all fours and ran North in a quick, easy pace I knew I could keep up for hours. As I ran through the bare trees, the wind called and cried, but I deafened my ears to it. I hurried, and shivered under my fur as I ran, for the first time in my life uncomfortable and strange in this, my own land.

CHAPTER THREE

B Y EARLY AFTERNOON, ONLY ANOTHER hour or so of hard travel remained until I arrived at the narrow valley where Spider Old Woman made her home. I paused to soak my sore paws; the hard ground had not softened any with the coming of spring this desolate year. But the icy water made me move on despite my weariness.

And I still had not come up with anything to tell Spider Old Woman. I shrugged my shoulders. She would help or not. My mother had sent many gifts to the wise one over the years and my failure to do the same now was unlikely to change her feelings towards us. I hoped. If she chose to be offended, there would be little I could do; however, she had always seemed to me to be a practical person, so I had faith she would understand my decisions. All of them.

I arrived before I felt truly prepared for the meeting. I stood at the top of the hill leading down into the valley and gazed at the snug little house below. Thin flat rocks stacked head-high formed circular walls, a thick thatched roof covered them and smoke curled into the sky above all, whisked away by the shrieking wind. As I approached the door, it opened and Spider Old Woman stood before me, straight and tall, arms folded over her chest.

Her long black hair shot through with silver hung in a braid over one shoulder and down to her waist. Fine lines crossed her face. Less than one might expect, but a sign of her great age. She wore the same black, ankle-length dress I had always seen her in, bound at the waist with a wide white sash. A strange woman, and powerful beyond imagination. She had never done harm to me or my family, but the *pinang* under her control made me shudder with a nervous fear. Only a fool would come here uninvited.

"Well, come on then. Quickly now, girl; I don't want to leave the door open for too long. Who knows what might creep in?"

I changed shape and followed her into the dim one-room cottage. Long wooden benches lined the walls with baskets and bundles piled underneath. She gestured towards a bench away from the door and I sank into it, more exhausted from the trip than I had expected, grateful to be out of the wind.

"Sit, I started boiling water for tea a while ago. I expected you a tad earlier. Did your feet get tired?"

I waited while she took out two fired-clay cups, put a pinch of dried leaves in each and filled them almost to the brim with steaming hot water.

She handed one to me and I took it gingerly. We sat in silence for long minutes, me trying to frame my request for help and advice, her gazing into the fire, keeping her thoughts to herself.

"So, tell me how things have been. Has all been well?"

My tongue tangled in my mouth. How could she not know?

She continued. "How does the outland girl fare? Do you visit with her often?"

For a moment my mind lay blank like a field of newly fallen snow, and then I understood of whom she spoke.

My friend Maggie had crossed into the land, our world from her own, tempted by dreams and guided by Spider Old Woman and Coyote, the trickster. While here, Maggie defeated a twisted sorcerer who had trapped the people of one of our villages. Since the battle, Maggie and her dog Jack have visited often and we have become close friends.

"The last I saw of them, Maggie and Jack did well. But

I have been asleep for a long time, Grandmother." And if the crying wind blew across the entire land, I did not know if my friends would be able to cross from their world to ours. I shivered. The wind might even blow across their world. Wind knows no boundaries.

"That girl never comes to visit me." Spider Old Woman grumbled into her cup. "You'd think she might bother, once or twice, to come see an old woman who helped her."

I blinked, startled. "Grandmother," I spoke slowly, unsure of my words or how they would be received, "I believe Maggie may think you do not care for her company."

"What?" For the first time in my memory, possibly anyone's memory, the old woman looked surprised. "Why would she think that?"

"You can be... abrupt at times."

"Hmmph. I am not abrupt. I am simply honest. I get things done."

And now my opening lay before me, a door I had only to find the courage to step through. "Grandmother, I know you are wise and often can find answers to problems that confuse others."

She looked across the fire at me, her lips twisted up in a smile. "Spit it out girl. Why are you here?"

"The crying wind. I need to find a way to stop the wind. Can you make it stop, or tell me how to silence it?"

She laughed, deep and long. "I wondered who would come to me. I should have guessed you of all the children would be most curious. What will you trade me for my advice?"

I looked at the packed-dirt floor between my feet. "I apologize, Grandmother. I brought no gifts this time, only a promise of future service." She raised her eyebrows but said nothing. "My parents struggle to save those who live in our valley. They have no time at the present to gather new herbs or food to replace what I might have taken to bring with me. I am sorry."

"Your parents... what did they think of your visit here? I cannot believe your mother would ever let you come empty-handed." Her light voice made the piercing tone all the more sharp. She was right, of course. My family visited Spider Old Woman often and my father often teased my mother about the weight of the hamper she filled with honey and other treats for the elder.

"They..." I thought of the lie I had concocted while I traveled, then thought better of it. "They did not want me to come. They worry that the wind will harm me. They worry too much about everything. I only want to help. I came anyway, without telling them."

Spider Old Woman fed the fire another twig and I felt my face flush. "I know your parents well. Better than you think. If they are worried, it is only for love of you. But you know that, when you are not busy being the child you say you are not.

"I also know your parents must have given you much of your strength, much of their teaching. You know then that you must use the appropriate cure to fight each illness. So let us see if you are suited to be my tool to defeat this wrongness."

I jumped a little where I sat on the bench.

"Grandmother, I am not a wielder of pinang, I have only the gift of my shapes. I am not the right one for this. I have only come to ask you to help us."

She took my now empty cup from me and moved to a hanging basket. She rustled through packets, lifted one compact deerskin pouch after another.

"Here. This will do nicely."

She put a pinch of something into both cups, then poured the still hot water from the pot in the ashes over the powder, swirling the liquid to dissolve the powder thoroughly.

She thrust my cup back towards me. "Drink this."

I took the dark tisane from her, hesitated. The thick

steam tasted of smoke, of ashes, of something darker.

"You are ready or not, girl. It is your choice."

I would not fail, not back down now. I breathed out, then held the cup of foul-smelling liquid to my mouth and drank as quickly as I could. I finished and my mouth twisted with the taste.

She took the cup from my hand and replaced it with another.

"You'll want to rinse your mouth now, I'm sure."

Clear cold water had never tasted so sweet. I wiped my lips when I had emptied the second cup and looked across the fire at her. "Now what?"

She finished her own potion before she answered. "Now we wait to see if you are a suitable weapon for this task."

"I do not want to be a weapon for a sorceress," I murmured. "I am supposed to be a healer." But I could hear my voice slur as I slumped against the wall behind the bench.

I looked into the fire and without warning, the bright flames spread all around, engulfing me.

The voice of the wind, which the walls of Spider Old Woman's house had blocked, came to me clearly now, louder than ever before, distinct. I could faintly hear a voice, almost, but not quite make out the words, someone calling, searching, lost and separated.

A scene resolved before me, growing clear in the middle of the flame: A tall tan building, with covered windows and oddly dressed people walking by. A breeze stirred up tiny waves across a small pond with trees that grew around one side. Ducks paddled serenely through the murky water.

I had never seen this place. The vision did me no good. I could have wept with frustration, but knew tears would serve no purpose.

Then I saw the man. He did not look like anything special: young, plain face, a bit stout, with messy light-colored hair. I searched for anything around him, but my attention kept returning to him. I did not recognize this figure, but was certain I would know him again.

I blinked and the picture changed. A girl, the same I had seen in the fire at my parents' home, now ran down a dark hallway. Her filthy skirts flapped behind her. She called out a word, over and over, a word I couldn't hear clearly or understand. The boy, Tomás she had called him, raced behind her, caught her in his arms. She struggled against him and the flames of Spider Old Woman's fire covered them all.

I blinked again. I sat beside the embers of Spider Old Woman's fire, leaning against the wall. For the first time I became aware of a rock from the wall that dug painfully into the small of my back. I shifted to get away from the lump. My arms and legs had gone to sleep, the pricks and stabs as the blood resumed its flow causing me to wince with pain and aggravation.

"How long?" I croaked, my voice raspy.

The darkened shape across the room moved, became her familiar form. "A few hours, no longer."

"No longer?" I echoed, surprised. "It felt only moments."

She laughed, a dry, raspy sound. I wondered if her mouth felt as parched as mine from the tisane.

"You cannot trust time in visions, child. You cannot trust anything in visions, to be truthful."

"Then what purpose was served by my doing that, seeing them?" I cried.

"We have more information now than we did before; however, you must remember that what we see is only a fragment. We do not yet know the meaning of the events we witnessed."

She fed another twig into the fire and continued, "I watched with you, shared your vision, but I would ask you to tell me what you saw in your own words. Between the two of us we may yet find something to work with."

I spoke first about the last part of the vision, the part

that concerned me the most. "At the end there was a girl in long skirts, running from a boy and then he caught her and she fought him." My words stumbled. "I think... I think I have seen them before, a few days ago."

"You have?"

"The first day my family woke from winter and found the wind around us. I was cooking, watching the flames and I wondered if I had only dreamed about them, the strange boy and the girl."

"Most interesting. You may be a promising tool indeed, if you are subject to visions naturally."

She reached over and refilled my water cup.

"Did you tell your parents?"

"Of course not! That was only a dream."

"Well, then. We shall put that piece of information aside for now. What did you think of the first part of the vision?"

"The man. I was drawn to him, but I know I have never met him. I do not know why my focus kept returning to him." I thought back to the strange scene. Something about the people felt familiar. "And I've never seen that place before, not the building, nor the pond edged with trees. The people looked strange as well, but something..." I trailed off, thinking.

"Of course!" I pushed to my feet in excitement. "The clothing—that is why the people looked familiar."

Spider Old Woman waited.

"The clothing from the first part of the vision is the same type as Maggie wears." I felt proud to have solved the riddle, then the import of my words struck me and I sank back down to the bench.

"Does that mean... ?"

"We do not know what anything means, child. Do not fret yourself yet." She pulled blankets out of a chest behind her and passed them to me. "Sleep now. I will think on this and decide what must be done."

"Grandmother, do you not need to sleep as well?"

I heard her laugh as she banked the fire. "Child, I do not remember the last time I slept. I doubt anyone does. As you get older, you need less sleep to get by. And I am very, very old."

That was true. Reminded of her years and her wisdom, I pushed away my worries and drifted to sleep with the voice of the wind crying softly in the night.

CHAPTER FOUR

ORNING IN SPIDER OLD WOMAN'S house came tinged with cold and I reached over from the bench on which I had slept to stir up the banked fire.

Her voice came from the shadows. "Leave it. I am still considering possibilities. It is easier to watch threads spin the future from a dark corner."

I had become accustomed to her puzzling speech and did not struggle to understand her so early in the morning. Instead I pushed myself upright on the bench and stretched.

The wind still howled. A secret corner of my heart had hoped that perhaps while I slept, Spider Old Woman had discovered the solution, had solved the problem and I could go home to my parents with an answer to trade against their night of worry.

But the crying wind answered that question.

Spider Old Woman spoke again. "About the second part of the vision, the fragments you see of the girl and the boy. I believe that to be an echo, part of a message perhaps, a cry for help or a scream of rage. We cannot tell. But behind the cry is a terrible wrongness, a heart in terror, in pain."

She paused.

"And it has found a way to reach us here."

Her words spilled over me like icy water.

"Reach us?" I echoed.

"Pay attention, girl. The wind comes from outside. The

force of that heart's anguish has broken our boundaries, swept our land. Perhaps the caller seeks help from us, but the words of the message have been lost over the distance."

My thoughts spun like Spider Old Woman's spindle. Outside? Then where? My heart sank. "The place in Maggie's world?"

"I do not know if that is where the problem is but you must start your search there."

"My search? Grandmother, I cannot go to that place. That is not my world. How can one of our people go into that strange place?"

"Your friend Ash goes back and forth as he wills and no harm comes to him. You will be safe enough."

I shook my head. The human boy Ash lived in a village nearby, and though we were close in age, I had always been amazed at his bravery. "Ash is different than I. He is not afraid. And he understands the speech of that people; I do not."

"Ash does not understand their speech, but thank you for reminding me. I'll need to make you a charm."

"What do you mean, Ash does not understand them? He talks with Maggie all the time." My voice faded to a whisper. "I talk with Maggie."

I gazed at where she sat in shadow, my mind now blank.

"You speak with her, but neither of you understand her language, nor does she truly understand ours. Coyote touched her, so that she understands, so that her tongue shapes our words, without her even thinking about the matter." She chuckled.

"Ask her some time about when she first met Ash by the river. They did not understand each other at all."

"Coyote," I said, desperate for another answer. "What about him? He travels back and forth between the worlds, Maggie says she has seen him there, even when she was awake. Why can he not go?"

Spider Old Woman shook her head. "Old Coyote is

wilder than ever in recent days, far from human, further from understanding human love and loss than ever before. And I believe that understanding will be the key to this problem."

"If you understand, why can you not... ?" I trailed off, blushing as I stared into her face.

She cocked her head to the side, one eyebrow raised. "I seldom leave my valley except through visions and dreams, child. You know that. Besides, I have tried to touch the source of the wind, but it will take an actual presence, more than I can bring to bear in that world."

Still, I cannot go, I thought. My parents need me here. But did they really? In the long run, that would help them more than any plants I could collect, more than any firewood I could gather. I thought of my father's stumble, thought of how I must not fail them.

So what prevented me from going? I sat, turned the question over in my mind, not liking the answer I found, but discovering no other.

I was afraid.

After all of my attempts to be an adult, after thinking it was time for me to live on my own, for my parents to not treat me as a child, it came down to fear. The taste of that knowledge was bitter.

I forced my eyes to meet those of Spider Old Woman. "What do I need to do?"

"I do not know, child." Her soft voice was like a hunter who feared to startle a deer. "I think once you find the place of the vision, you will be led to the answer." She stirred up the fire, casting flares of light and shadow across her face. "I know what I ask is not easy for you; however, I have faith in you and your abilities. Your heart is stronger than you know. It will serve you well."

I started for home in the late morning, the pouch holding

the charm of language pressed tightly around my neck under my fur. Spider Old Woman had said it would not interfere with everyday language, that its magic was strong enough to stay with me through my changes. I could feel its power squirm against my chest, settling deeper into my breastbone, nesting inside of me. As I ran across the bleak grasslands I worried about the next challenge I faced: my parents.

I reached home before they returned from their rounds and hastened to prepare the evening meal, guilt nipping at my steps. My father unsealed the cliff side, then froze at the door. My mother pushed past him and wrapped her arms around me. After a moment he enclosed us both in his grip.

"Never again, daughter. Never again. Please. We cannot stand the fear, not knowing what has become of you."

I was a coward. For the rest of the evening I said nothing of the mission Spider Old Woman had entrusted to me, let my parents pet and coddle me. I tidied our home, checked on the supplies, collected firewood, and performed all my normal chores, making sure to not be out of their sight for any longer than necessary.

That night I lay sleepless, listening to their soft breathing, more ragged, more tired than I remembered. Finally I changed back into human form and sat by the fire, my hands wrapped tightly around the charm that hung from my neck, as if by force of will I could press it out of existence; push this task onto another.

Dawn came and my father found me sitting by the remains of the fire.

"Daughter, when are you planning to tell us?"

I sat upright, startled. "Tell you what?"

"I do not know. But it is clear to both your mother and me that something has happened."

I felt my throat close. I had thought I was protecting them and all the time they knew. "Let's wait for Mother to wake and then we can talk about it together."

Father laughed. "She already lays awake waiting, cub. We decided you would talk more readily to one of us at a time. I will get her."

I wiped my face on my hands and gathered my words while I waited for them to return.

"You must know I went to visit Spider Old Woman." I looked over at them. My father's face was a riddle to me, my mother looked away. "In truth, I think it was good for me to have gone. While there, Spider Old Woman gained knowledge about the wind that brings the sickness. She believes it may be a cry for help."

My parents looked at each other, a glance full of questions, but did not interrupt.

"She says the only way to stop the wind, to save our people, is for me to go find the source of it. To answer the cry."

I stopped. Little else remained to be said, besides the last part.

My mother asked the question I dreaded. "Where does she say you need to go?"

I answered slowly. "First I will go to the village to the South and West of us, the one Ash comes from."

My father nodded. "That is good. I have worried about the people there."

"I will not stay there, Father. I will go from there to where Spider Old Woman says the cry echoes from." I swallowed. "She believes it comes from the other world, the one the girl Maggie comes from."

"No!" Shrill, my mother's voice rang from the cavern's roof. "No, you cannot go. Not to the land of the strange ones." Her hands fluttered. "The girl is nice enough, I grant you. I like the girl. But you cannot go to her land. They are not our people, their ways not ours. How can Grandmother ask this of you?"

My father sat silent, watching me.

"Mother, if I do not go, if the wind continues, what will happen to our people? What will happen to our land, if the wind blows for another week, another month, another year?"

She shook her head, eyes wide. "We will find a way. We will learn to live with it, discover a cure."

I shook my head. "You and Father are the wisest healers I know. If you have not discovered a cure for this sickness by now, there is none. You would not be stopped by any mortal illness. But you will exhaust yourselves trying to find a cure, trying to care for those who are afflicted and in so doing, weaken yourselves. You would have me stay here, helpless and watch you both fade away. I cannot do that. I am sorry."

We sat in silence, huddled each in our own misery, until my father spoke. "She must go. For us to keep her here is selfish; it harms her and our people. And she is right; we are no closer to a cure than on the first day. This must end." He put his arm around my mother's shuddering shoulders and she buried her face in his chest.

I left the next morning, having spent the night in preparation for the journey. I had made the trip to the village several times by myself over the last summer and fall. Two days of easy walking, easier yet in bear shape.

"I'll keep an eye out along the way, see what herbs I can bring back," I told my mother. "If nothing else, this is a chance to replenish our stock without further depleting the valley."

She smiled, only a little too brightly and packed more things into the hamper. This argument I had lost. I wanted to travel light, carry nothing and leave them as much of the larder as possible. Both had dismissed that notion, with a tone of finality that made it clear I should not argue any further.

I shifted shapes and Mother adjusted the straps that held the basket to my back. I kept myself from telling her I could do it myself. Let her have one more thing to do.

I hugged her and turned to my father. Even in his human shape, the strength in his arms and the force of his embrace always surprised me.

"Go quickly and safely. Return soon."

I left the cave at a trot, only stopping once to turn and wave before I set my face to the South and West towards Ash's village. I noted new patches where herbs and plants struggled against the wind. If all went well I would collect them on my way home. Young prickly-pear joints and yucca shoots for rheumatism. Sage for fever and aches. Coneflower root for toothache. The land had always given us what we needed to care for our people. I worried what would happen if true spring never came, if the herbs we must pick in full bloom never flowered.

As late afternoon wore on I worried about finding a likely place to sleep. Normally I curled up anywhere I chose, but with the howling wind as my constant companion I decided I would be more comfortable in a sheltered spot. On my trips south I had seen a particular outcropping of rock I thought would serve as a shelter. I remembered it lay not much further.

I remembered wrong. Darkness fell before I found the landmark I searched for. Exhausted, I shoved the basket in a crevasse in the rocks, changed my form to the smaller one, and then crawled into the open space after it. I pulled blankets out to block gaps in the stones and shivered at the sound.

The wind howled around me. Now that I was not running, I was free to listen to it, would I or not. Now that I had seen the girl, seen her chased by the boy, I imagined I could hear her voice on the wind, hear her begging for help.

There would be no way to sleep through this. I tossed

and turned. Finally I thought of a way to block the sound. I scrounged for tufts of new grass and twisted them tightly. I carefully placed one in each ear. The plugs helped somewhat and I curled up tight in my fur and tried to sleep.

I slept fitfully and in the morning I ached in places I could not ease, no matter how I stretched. After a cold breakfast, I changed back and shrugged on the basket. The long night had only reinforced my desire to be rid of the wind. Even if Spider Old Woman was correct, if there was no malice in the cry, it was terrible and had to be stopped.

By early afternoon the walls of the village rose before me. Blocks of terraced buildings with ladders bridging each story and narrow pathways between the buildings greeted me. But I heard none of the expected sounds of village life over the wind. Nothing moved in the narrow streets. Besides the ever-present wind, the village lay before me quiet, unearthly.

I entered the streets and before I had gone far, a young boy peered over a corner of the roof and shrieked.

I cursed and changed my shape. Most of Ash's people had seen me before, but apparently not this one. An older child, perhaps the first one's sister, leaned over the edge of the roof.

"Go away! You're not wanted here!"

I looked up, confused by their hostility. "I'm here to see Ash. Is he here, visiting his mother?" Lately Ash spent most of his time in the village, but he sometimes returned to his little hut made out of pine branches up on the hillside.

The girl frowned. "How do you know Ash?"

I sighed. "He and I are friends. Would you come down so we could talk about this, or could I come up?"

She shrugged and then lowered the ladder to me.

I adjusted the straps of the basket and climbed, careful

not to tangle my feet in the hem of my coat on the rungs.

Once on the roof, the girl faced me, arms folded over her skinny chest. "You're one of the Bear People, yes?"

I nodded.

"Are you a healer, then?"

I hesitated. "I have worked with my parents, yes. I am in training to be a healer."

She bit her lips. "You will have to do."

She went down the ladder to the interior of the building. I shrugged, confused, and followed her down.

High slitted windows did little to relieve the shadows of the room, but enough light filtered in for me to see a row of people stretched out on thin mattresses, wasted and thin.

"What has happened here?" I whispered.

"We think it is the wind. They fall sick and are hot to the touch, and will not wake." She looked at me. "Our healer was one of the first to fall. Will you help us?"

I looked at the fever tossed forms and knew I could give only one answer.

"I will do my best."

CHAPTER FIVE

T HE DAY WAS ENDLESS. I found a small group of young adults and children who were unaffected by the wind, who had not fallen weak at its cry. I used them mercilessly to fetch and heat water, find fresh blankets, make poultices and tisanes.

I did not spare myself. The boy who first saw me became my guide and led me from one darkened room to another, each one occupied by the sick ones, as they lay listlessly on their beds. The children followed me as I examined each patient, left instructions with a young assistant or a family member if I could find a healthy one and moved on.

To pass between buildings, the children showed me a system of tunnels carved from the bedrock countless years before. I had never known they existed, not in all the times I had visited Ash. Now I was grateful. Every trip below ground provided a respite from the sobbing wind. We began the slow process of relocating the ill down below. They did not improve, but did not weaken further.

Still, I had not visited some sections of the village yet and somewhere, in a tiny dark room, I feared to find my friend.

My parents had told me when a healer is truly working, when there is a crisis among the people, you have no friends, no enemies, only patients. You sort them, determine the extent of their injury or illness, do your best for each and move on. There is no time, no energy, for anything more personal than that.

I did not believe them when they told me this. I laughed and said I would spend extra time with my friends. I would sit by their bed, even when I wasn't needed and make sure they knew I cared for them. As a child, I had frowned to think of curing enemies. Wouldn't it be better to let them die?

But now I knew better. You cannot spare the energy to decide who to treat. All are simply bodies before you, bodies that do not work the way they should and all you can do is your best to make them well. Anything else, any other thoughts, simply must wait.

And so I did not rush to my friend, ask where I could find him, did not do more than wonder if he was in the village, or alone in his small house. By nightfall I could no longer move, could not climb up or down another ladder. I sat next to the fire, yet felt no warmth. I tried to shift into the warmer bear shape, but could not hold the image in my mind long enough to complete the transition. I lay still and gazed into the fire.

Isabel stood slightly behind a man dressed in a brown loose robe belted with leather. She clutched at the squirming Nicco, as if desperate to keep the large cat out from under foot and more importantly, away from sharp hooves.

"Tell your people to bring my men five bags of corn and some water for our horses," the leader of the horsemen snapped, not even pausing to dismount. His sun-wrinkled face stared over their heads, as if he already had passed through, was already gone.

The man in the brown robe ignored the rudeness. "Captain, these people are under the protection of the Church. They provide service for the mission and as such are exempt from tribute, as you well know."

The captain slapped the dusty brown neck of his horse, then swung his leg over and dismounted, signaling the rest of his men to do the same.

"This isn't tribute, Brother, just a polite request for resupply. We're on our way east, out to the far mesa. The Brother stationed there sent a message with one of his faithful; they're having trouble with those dances and masks and what not again." He brushed a layer of dust off his buckskin leggings, then straightened. "I would have thought you would want to support us ridding the pueblos of the devil dancers."

"So, this is merely a request?"

The captain lightly touched the sling from which a long dagger hung. "Exactly, Brother Alonzo. A request."

Brother Alonzo gestured for one of the older village men to come forward and take the captain's horse. Others came and held the bridles for the rest of the soldiers' mounts and led the horses off to drink.

"Request or not, we cannot give you five bags of grain. My children here are hungry and the harvest has been poor. I fail to understand why you could not have been bothered to carry enough with you."

The captain laughed. "Why should we bother, old man. There are villages aplenty to supply us on the road. Besides," he leered over Fray Alonzo's shoulder to where Isabel stood. "It seems you have plenty of food to keep some extra comforts about." Her cheeks flushed and Fray Alonzo stepped forward, towards the captain, who continued on, disregarding the angry set of the other man's jaw. "You can always eat that cat if you get hungry enough. He looks big enough to provide a dinner for half the mission."

Isabel stepped from behind the shelter of the priest, eyes blazing, hand wrapped fiercely in Nicco's black-and-white fur. "Nicco at least serves a purpose in keeping the mice from our corn as it dries. It's a pity he can't protect us from all thieves and beggars."

The man's face darkened and he raised his hand to the girl.

"Enough!" Fray Alonzo boomed. "Captain, your horses are watered." He pointed behind the company where a large group of men from the village stood, holding the horses. *"You should go now. There is nothing for you here."*

The captain and his men swung up into their saddles and whirled their mounts around. *"I'll be sure to tell Governor Otermin about your lack of cooperation today. We shall see what happens the next time you call for help when the Apache threaten to raid."*

The company galloped away and didn't hear Fray Alonzo's shout to the sky. *"Nothing, that's what will happen. And the Apache wouldn't raid if you would stop attacking them for slaves!"* Fray Alonzo lowered his fist. *"Mongrel dogs, every one of them."*

And then he looked at where Isabel stood behind him with wide eyes and his face softened.

"I'm sorry, child. Of course I don't mean that about you. Come on," he laid a hand on her thin shoulder, *"let's go inside and see what can be done about dinner tonight."* He scratched behind Nicco's ear and was rewarded by licks from a bright pink tongue. *"Put that beast down and let him do his work, now that you've so admirably defended him and his position with us."*

"Bear Girl? Are you all right?" Ash knelt over me.

"My apologies. I merely became tired." My mind caught up with me. "I thought you must be here, but there are so many people..." My voice faded out and I leaned into his chest, just for a moment, just to rest.

He patted my hair awkwardly. "I am fine. The wind tires me, but I am not sick, not like some of the others here." He looked down.

"What is it?"

"My mother. When you can, will you come see her?"

I closed my eyes, gathered what strength remained

in me.

"I will come now. Show me the way."

———— ⊁—— ⊁——— ⊁——— ⊁—— ⊁

Ash carried my basket with its sorely depleted contents and threw my coat over his arm. He led me through the tunnels, then up into a room that was empty save for one figure who lay quiet. Strands of her gray hair pulled out from the thick braid to lay loose upon the pillow.

When I finished my examination of Ash's mother I turned to him and motioned that we should step outside of the room.

He grabbed my arm. "What is it? What is wrong?" His white face looked ghostly in the shadows.

I shook him off and whispered, "Outside now, please."

On the roof the wind howled. "I have done what I can for your mother. She is not in any immediate danger, though she should be below with the others."

"Why are we here?" he waved his arms around the rooftop. "I believed you wanted us to stay out of the wind as much as we are able to."

"What do you hear?" I had begun to have suspicions about the cause of the illness, but wanted to mull over what it might mean.

Ash frowned. "I don't hear anything clearly."

I pressed him. "What does the wind sound like to you?"

After a moment he answered. "Voices. Or a voice. It is hard to tell." He shook his head. "I think it is a voice, calling for someone. Sometimes I think I recognize the voice, but I don't know who it is."

"Who do you think it sounds like?" I was curious to see if his answer lined up with my suspicions, but I did not wish to reveal my thoughts, not yet.

"Sometimes I think I hear my mother calling." He blushed. "Sometimes the voice sounds more like Maggie."

Interesting. I wondered which voice he found more

43

embarrassing to tell me. But the other girl's name reminded me of my mission.

I gestured for us to return inside. After a quick stop to adjust his mother's blankets, we returned to the silent room in which he had found me before.

"Ash, I didn't come to the village for the reasons I usually do, just to visit or trade."

He shrugged. "I did think this an odd time for you to be traveling. But I did not think to ask. We needed you and you appeared. I do not know what we would do if you were not here."

I squirmed. "That is part of the problem. I need to leave."

He stared at me. "You cannot! There are people here that depend on you. My mother..." His voice choked.

I ran my hands through my hair. "Ash, you must believe me. There is nothing I have been doing to help anyone, even your mother, which I cannot train you or any other healthy person to do. All that can be done is keep the afflicted comfortable and wait."

"Wait for what?"

I looked away from the village, into the night. "Wait for me to leave, so I can complete the task laid upon me. Wait and hope."

I told him of my meeting with Spider Old Woman and my need to cross over to Maggie's world to find the source of the wind.

He stared at me. "How long will you be gone?"

I threw my hands into the air. "I do not know anything about it. How can I? I have never been to the other world. I came here because I wanted your assistance. And now I do not know what to do."

My exhaustion returned in full force and I leaned against the wall.

Ash gazed at me, his face grave. "Give me three days."

"What?"

"Three days and then I will guide you to Maggie's world.

I do not know what good my assistance will be, but you will have it. But first, stay here with my people for three more days and see if there are any you can save."

———— ✳ — ✳ — ✳ — ✳ — ✳

I spent the days training more assistants. As I suspected, the younger adults were less likely to have succumbed to the voices of the wind. In conversations with the families of the afflicted, I came to understand all those who now lay motionless, or tossed in fever-filled dreams, had heard the voice of loved ones calling them. But unlike Ash, the loved ones they heard were all lost. Long ago or recent, it made no difference. In every case of illness, I discovered the voices of their dead called to them.

Mid-afternoon of the third day arrived and I sat and sorted through a final pile of herbs gathered by my helpers.

I had not spoken to Ash further about when we would depart. I knew he did not want to leave the side of his mother even though he knew there would be little he could do to ease her.

A thin girl tumbled down the ladder. "Healer, healer! Your friend is coming!"

I looked up, confused, then climbed the ladder after her and tried to focus my eyes in the bright sun to follow where she pointed.

In the distance I could see someone approaching, braced against the wind as if expecting a physical blow. At first I thought a strange boy had come, then recognized the tall girl with light-brown hair, dressed in boy's clothing, walking beside a medium-sized, black-and-white dog.

"Maggie!" I shouted and waved my arms over my head.

She glanced up and gave a little wave, then wrapped her arms around her body and shuffled further down the trail towards the village.

Ash reached Maggie before I did. By the time I met with them on the trail they had nearly reached the village. His arm wrapped tightly around her shoulders and she kept one arm at his waist, as if holding herself up only by force of will.

Ash helped her towards the ladder and I turned to Jack. The dog sat before me, ears up, tail sweeping large arcs into the dust.

I reached over and scratched behind his ears. "It is good to see you as well, but we should go in."

He trotted before me through the streets of the village. "Jack, wait!"

The dog stopped and looked at me over his shoulder, with a clear expression of "now what?"

"We all need to go inside. I do not know if the wind will harm you as well, but I would feel better if you joined us." I moved towards the ladder. "I will help you, if you would like."

He gave me a wide grin and his tongue lolled out. Then he continued in the direction he had been heading before I called and went around a corner.

"Wait!" I scrambled to follow him and found him scratching up a flat stone. Beneath it were a set of neatly folded buckskins. Jack turned to me and raised the marks on his forehead that were placed just where eyebrows would have been.

Oh.

"I am sorry, Jack. I was not thinking."

Face burning, I went back around the corner and waited.

In a few moments, a wiry dark-haired young man came out from the alley the dog had gone down, a broad grin on his face. Jack poked me in the ribs. "You need a nap, or some coffee, or something. Of all people, I didn't expect you to forget."

I had been there when the sorcerer whom Maggie fought last summer tried to trap her in another shape. Jack had been caught in the spell by mistake, turning him into a young boy. Only by luck and determination had we been able to get him to safety and only by the good graces of Spider Old Woman and Coyote was he now able to change shapes as he liked.

Unlike me, his fur did not stay with him. I should have remembered he needed a few moments of privacy to change forms and cover himself. I shook my head.

"Come on. Maggie will be wondering where we are."

CHAPTER SIX

"**W**HAT IS GOING ON HERE?" Maggie's teeth chattered as she rummaged through her ever-present backpack, finally pulling out a large scarf, wrapping it like a blanket over the long shirt she already wore.

"What is that wind?" She stopped, face pale. "Is he out? My dreams were so odd. Did he escape?"

Ash shook his head, grabbed her arms to calm her.

"No, Maggie. Shriveled Corn Man is still locked away. There is more than one danger that roams here."

Maggie's shoulders sagged in relief. I understood her fear. This wind did harm, but Spider Old Woman felt the illness was something in the nature of an incidental side effect. Shriveled Corn Man had been full of malice and hatred and a twisted madness.

"Come, let us sit and talk." I led them away, not to one of the underground storage rooms, far from the wind, but a high chamber. I wanted light, light to see the faces of my companions as I told the story as I knew it so far. We sat in a small adobe apartment. The building was constructed so that most of the windows faced other buildings around an enclosed courtyard. Light came in but the courtyard was not large enough for the wind to blow into our little refuge with any true force.

Maggie looked at me, brow furrowed, then sat on a folded blanket. Ash sat near her. Jack stayed in a corner, in what shadows remained, leaning against some old sacks.

I wished he would come and join us, but something in his posture made me leave him alone, focus my attention away from him and onto Maggie.

"Maggie," I started then stopped. How to best explain my mission from Spider Old Woman? Her words had been so vague, but her intent definite.

"First, what did you mean by 'odd dreams'?"

She shook here head. "It hasn't been like before, when Coyote was playing games. For the last week, every time I woke up I thought I could hear someone calling me, like when you can hear someone talking, but can't quite make out the words. This morning it was so strong I couldn't think of anything else but to see if it was from here."

Ash and I looked at each other and shrugged. "We have not called you, but we do need your help. This wind has blown across the land for weeks. Spider Old Woman believes the source of the wind comes from your world."

Maggie sat up straight, tilted her head. "My world? But how could anything there affect the weather, the wind here?"

I shrugged. "When I visited Spider Old Woman, she caused me to have two visions. The people in the first dressed much as you do. It could have been a scene from your home village, or any other in your world." I paused. "There have been other visions as well, but Spider Old Woman thought they are echoes from something else, possibly confusing the message."

Ash interrupted. "But I thought your family did not hold more pinang than the shape change? Not," he hurried to add, "that I believe that to be an easy thing. But you have never mentioned holding magic before."

"I do not," I said through gritted teeth. "Only what I was born to. I want no magic. I will be no sorceress, but a healer, as I have been trained."

Ash frowned at my words. How could he understand? He was found, brought to the village as a child and though none held that against him, he could not understand how important it was for me to follow in the steps of my family, to do as my people have always done.

Maggie's lips pursed and she looked worried. "Visions, where you see what's going on? Or dreams, where people speak with you?"

"Visions. I watch only. A girl, a boy and a man in a strange robe and other men on horses and..." I laughed. "A very large, fluffy black-and-white cat." I glanced over to where Jack sat in the shadows. "You and he would make a fine pair."

He snorted and I continued my story.

"And then another place is tied in to all of this somehow." A hopeless request, to ask her to find a place I had glimpsed once in a vision and only briefly.

Maggie nodded. "Tell me and I'll let you know if I've seen it." She brightened. "Even if it's not in Albuquerque, I might have seen something about the place on television or in a movie, or if it's someplace famous that gets used a lot. Or..." Her voice faded as Ash and I stared at her.

"Um, right. So, just tell me what the people looked like and I'll do my best."

I closed my eyes, ignored the whispers of the wind outside, sought to pull the image from my mind, to see it clearly again. "Men and women walk around, in a wide variety of clothing. Many wear blue pants like yours, though some women wear skirts and both wear shorter pants. Both the men and women wear their hair long and short and some of them have colors in their hair, blue or green or even white, even though they do not look old." I opened my eyes.

"I am sorry, I know this sounds absurd, but it is what they looked like."

Maggie shrugged. "It sounds pretty normal. Not much to go on for figuring out the place, but you're right, that's probably my world."

I blinked and wondered about her world and how strange it must be. Why wonder, I thought. Soon enough I would go see for myself. My stomach knotted.

I closed my eyes again, tried to find more details for her to use to identify the scene. "The people walk on hard stone paths and in the middle of the paths there is a grassy area, very green, and people lay or sit on the grass and they talk, but some of them have those book things, like you showed us in the fall."

Maggie interrupted. "School books, or just regular books?"

I shrugged, my eyes still closed. "What is the difference? They look much like what you showed us after your school started, thick and bulky.

"Large buildings sit across the green grass and shaped something like the buildings of the village, but too tall, too solid, not right.

"And in the middle of the green area there is a little pond, with a tiny island in it. Trees grow closely on one side of the pond and a rock juts out into the water from beneath them.

"A flock of ducks swims through the water, though it is not very clean-looking water, and chase each other for scraps of bread."

Jack laughed.

"Jack, what's so funny?" Maggie's voice was sharp.

"Don't you get it? Where she's describing?"

Maggie sighed. "No, I don't, not yet. But I'm sure I'll think of something."

"Jack," I cut in. "Do you know where this is?"

"Sure. So does Maggie."

She glared at him.

"Ducks, in a pond. With students on the grass and buildings all around. Maggie, it's the duck pond at the university where Dad works."

She gasped. "You're right. You've got to be right." Then

she looked quizzically at Jack. "How can you remember that? They've only let me take you a couple times."

He grinned. "Ducks. I tend to remember places with ducks."

Now we had a starting place, a beginning to the thread.

"Maggie, will you go with me to this place? And help me as I work?"

"Of course I will," she responded.

Jack shook his head. "Sorry, but you can't."

"What do you mean? I'm helping," she broke off and her eyes widened. "Oh, no."

My heart sank.

She said in a quiet low voice, "Bear Girl, I can only help in the afternoons, maybe only for an hour or two each day. School is in session now. The only reason I can stay here so long is that time moves differently in this place. I can be here for days and only a little time has passed at home."

Maggie's face brightened again. "It's Sunday afternoon now. If you could wait a few more days, it would be the weekend again and I could help."

I shook my head. "Thank you. But I need to go as soon as possible and with the difference in time between our worlds, that might be weeks here. If I have not found anything on my own by the time you can help me, I will gladly accept."

Two things now to make my heart sink further. I would be on my own and I would have to move even more quickly than I had imagined. While I did not know exactly how the time difference worked, if every hour in Maggie's world counted for several here, my time would be limited indeed.

I shook my head, as upset by the idea of working alone as the issue with the time.

Ash spoke up. "I told you I would go with you, Bear Girl."

I glanced at him. His face was set, hard. I knew what this would cost him. I feared to be alone in that strange world, but... "Ash, I release you from your promise. I know where to go now. You could not help me there further. You would be much more assistance here, making sure all stays well with the village."

A mixture of guilt and relief crossed his face and after a moment, he nodded in agreement.

So, that was that. I would leave and go on my own.

"I'll go with you."

The voice from the shadowed corner startled me from my black mood.

"Jack?" Maggie's wide eyes betrayed her shock.

I turned and looked at him.

He shrugged. "I don't need to be in school, there's not much for me to do here, and it's sort of boring sitting around waiting for you to come home." His look became challenging. "Why shouldn't I go help her?"

Maggie blinked. "It's not safe! And how can you help her? You don't know the city either."

"I know it better than he does," Jack pointed with his chin towards Ash, "and I'm the one who recognized the duck pond. I do watch where we're going when we're out."

"Yes, you watch because you want to stick your head out of the window!"

Jack's eyes narrowed. "I watch because I'm interested. There's not a lot for me to do there. Traveling, doing things, is exciting. What do you think I do all day when you're gone?"

"I don't know, I'm gone!"

"You could have asked. It's not like it would have been hard for you to ask me now."

Maggie looked down.

I stared between the two of them. I had never dreamed to see them quarrel like this. Jack looked different somehow, but in the poor light and in my tired state of mind I could not put my finger on what exactly.

"I wait. I sleep on the bed, because there's nothing else

to do. There's no one to let me in and out, so I can't even check out to see if anything is going on in the yard. Every day, for hours, I wait.

"And now, there's something I can do to help, something that would be useful, and you don't want me to?" Jack's voice lowered. "Let me ask you one thing, Maggie. Do you still think you own me?"

Maggie's face paled.

"Of course I don't own you. But you're still my, oh, I don't know! I just don't want anything to happen to you. And I didn't know you were so unhappy, I didn't."

Tears ran down her cheek and she dashed them away furiously.

Jack's voice softened. "I'm not unhappy when we're off doing things. I'm not. But I'm different now. I didn't mind waiting so much before last summer, but the more time I spend as a boy, the more I think like a human. Dogs don't have much of a sense of time. We get bored, sure, but it usually doesn't wear on and on. Imagine if you were locked up in the same place for eight hours, every day. You can't read, you can't watch television, there's no one to talk to, nothing to do, but sleep and stare out the window and wait to be rescued. And you know that even if you're rescued, you'll be locked up again the next day."

He looked away. "Everything is different now; I don't know how to explain it. But I didn't mean to upset you. I guess we should have talked about this a long time ago."

Maggie crawled over to where he sat and hugged him. "I'm sorry. I should have thought about how this would change things. When you're a boy, I do think of you as a boy. Even as a dog, you're still my kid brother. I'd do anything to keep you from being unhappy."

She sat back on her heels, face set. "And that also means doing anything to keep you safe. I don't know what is going on, I don't know who Bear Girl is going to fight and I don't want you to go with her. What if something were to happen to you? How would I..." she stopped, hair over her face and ducked her head.

Jack patted her head and looked over her bent back to me, as if seeking advice. I wanted nothing more than to keep out of this argument, but knew that was the coward's road.

"Maggie, look at me." She sniffled, then looked up. "I do not want to put Jack in any danger either. I do not know where I will be going or whom I will be facing. If I understand correctly, Jack will only be able to be in his dog form in your world, yes?"

She nodded and straightened a little more.

"Could he at least guide me to the pond?"

Maggie thought, nodded again.

She turned to Jack. "Would that be okay?"

He shrugged.

"If you tell me how to find your home, I will make sure to bring him back safely after he shows me the pond."

I turned to Jack, who had retreated into the shadows. "If this is agreeable to you, I would value your companionship, Jack."

Once the decision had been made Maggie became a whirl of activity. She pulled out a book of paper from her backpack and started making lists.

"To get there, you'll need to take the bus. Heck, you can't take the bus with Jack. I have some money saved up, so you can take a taxi to the duck pond while you have him and afterwards, you can use the bus. I'll need to get you some bus maps and notes about the city."

I hated to stop her, but had to ask. "Maggie, do you have such a map with you?" She looked confused. "I do not know if I can read your writing. My people do not write; I do not know if it would be useful to have this map."

Her shoulders fell, then she took on a look

of determination.

"I'll draw cards for you with the bus numbers and you can match the pictures and when you get on just tell the driver where you want to go."

"Maggie? I'm sure this will work." I paused, not wishing to appear foolish. "But tell me, what is a bus?"

CHAPTER SEVEN

As THE DAY WORE ON Jack and Maggie left us to fetch me clothing and other things I would need. Jack had not spoken since their fight.

I spent the rest of the day preparing my young assistants as best as I could, then paced the roughly carved underground tunnels, helpless, unsure of what I could do while I waited.

Ash found me there.

"Bear Girl, what can I do? How can I help?"

I stopped, stared blankly. "I want more than anything to go to my family, to tell them what I have found here, that I am all right." I closed my eyes. "And I can do none of that." I opened my eyes again. "So, what I want will wait."

Ash smiled. "This, at least, I can do. You altered your plans so I would be able to remain with my mother during her illness. I can make the trip to your family's home. I will leave now while you are still here and then be back quickly."

My chest relaxed; I felt as if I had just now taken my first full breath in days.

"Please. Tell them we have a good plan and..."

Ash laughed.

I smiled back. "You and I know our plan is not complete, or even truly started. But they do not need to know that. Tell them I am fine and will return as soon as I can."

After he left, I sat in the room where the four of us had made our plans. If Spider Old Woman was right, I could not afford to waste the chance for another clue.

———✶——✶——✶——✶——✶———

Isabel walked throughout the pathways of the pueblo as it spread out from the mission. An old man sat in the sun on a wooden stool, resting his back against the warm adobe wall of his home.

"Good morning, sir. Have you seen Tomás?"

The old man opened his eyes and smiled.

"Ah, daughter of my daughter. It is good to see you home."

Isabel squirmed. "I have been here for three years, grandfather."

"You have been in the mission for three years. And before that, you lived with your father, the Spaniard. He took a flower of our women for his wife and left for his ranch. My daughter never returned to us. You were born far away, child, but you are still a child of the people. Do not forget that."

Isabel said nothing, but looked past the man, over his head into the distance.

The old man sighed. "But you do not want to hear this. You think you are Spanish, all the way through. So be it. I will not tell you different."

Isabel flushed, lowered her eyes. "I do not deny my people, either of them. I do not see why it is important to make such a big concern of the past, that is all."

The old man shook his head. "I hope you never have to understand." He stood. "Tomás is speaking with some others. They are discussing things of the village and should not be disturbed."

Isabel's shoulders dropped and she turned to walk away.

"Do not go yet, child. Your mother was very gifted. She could see the other worlds, could talk with the spirits and they would hear her. We hope to see that in you, the talent

to see, to hear, to speak."

"Sir, I do not have such power. I have never heard anything I did not think was from this world."

He shook his head. "You may not have known what to listen for. I am sure Josefa did not teach you."

Isabel's back straightened. "Do not speak ill of my mother. She was a good woman and taught me much."

The old man slumped back down. "But my daughter did not teach my granddaughter everything she might need to face the coming years. And for that I am sorry."

"Isabel!" A younger man's voice rang out and she spun around towards the speaker.

Tomás ran towards her, grabbed her arm, bent his head low over hers as if to whisper...

The vision faded and I had no more information than before, only suspicions about the girl. I was sure somehow the wind centered on the girl, perhaps she was the one who caused it. I nodded, weighed the words in my mind. This made sense. I would go to Maggie's world, find the girl, discover why she had summoned the wind and then return home. This time I had tried to pay attention to her clothing, how she moved. Her long skirts and full blouses looked different from anything I'd ever seen Maggie wear. That would make her easier to find.

I knelt again before a thick, furry bundle. My coat.

Maggie had explained it would be impossible to wear my coat in public in her world; that people would rather believe I had killed the bear whose skin I wore than the truth.

I could not travel there in bear shape. And there would be no safe place to leave it. Maggie had offered to hide it in her room, but I worried her parents would come across it and questions would arise which she could not answer.

So it must stay here, safe in the keeping of Ash's people.

I did not worry about the coat, did not fear they would try to burn it to trap me, or other such foolishness. But I had never gone without it for so much as a day, much less left it somewhere. I gathered it in my arms to take to the chamber in which Ash's mother lay.

"Bear Girl?" Maggie's voice sounded soft as a whisper. I had not heard her or Jack enter the room behind me while I knelt there. "Are you going to be all right without your coat?"

I nodded, turned to face them. "I will be fine."

Maggie lay down the packs she carried, drew things out, then stopped. "I've always wondered... Do you mind if I ask?"

"I cannot imagine a question of yours bothering me, but ask what?"

She bit her lips together, then continued. "Are you a girl in a bear shape, or a bear who wears a girl shape?"

I stared at her for so long that she stuttered an apology.

"No, Maggie, I do not mind the question. It is simply I have never thought about it before. This is who I am, both shapes."

She looked down at her knees and I wondered if she was asking about me, or about Jack, who sat behind her, still silent.

Maggie identified the different items she brought, the maps, clothing and some slips of paper she said I would need to trade for food.

"I know this is a lot to learn all at once," she apologized.

I laughed. "My parents expect me to remember the seven uses of a plant after first being shown it. To be able to recite the eleven cures for a fever and to know where each cure can be found, in what season, and what part of the plant to use."

I waved my hand over the pile of objects. "This is new to me, yes and I do not always understand the reasoning. But do not fear my ability to remember what you teach me. You are far more patient than my parents."

"Probably because I'm in school, too, and know what it's like. Though... I could probably miss just a day or so. Other kids play hookey, skip school," she added, seeing my confusion, "all the time, and it would make this easier."

"No!" Jack's voice startled us both. "You will not skip school. You couldn't tell Mom and Dad why if they caught you. You know it's important to go. If it wasn't important, they wouldn't make you do it."

"He is right, Maggie. Your first instinct was that you could not go with me. Follow that instinct. There may be a reason for Jack and me to do this together."

Maggie forced a smile at Jack. "I'll have to act like you ran away for the afternoon if you're not back before they get home. You know they'll notice you missing."

Jack looked uncomfortable. "I don't want to make them worry. But we both know they'll worry a lot less about me being gone than they would about you."

An uncomfortable silence covered us all. As much as I did not want my friends to fight, I could not afford the time, either.

"Please, I think we have settled this, it is just that we are not completely happy with the answer. Let us continue with what I need to know."

Jack and I planned to leave as soon as we could. He left the room while I changed into the clothing Maggie had brought. She helped me with the new garments. The pants—— "jeans" she called them——bound my legs, tight and uncomfortable. Maggie laughed and said they fit well and were supposed to look as they did.

I seldom liked to wear leggings at all; these felt terrible. She showed me the new shoes, tight around my feet, with soles so thick I tripped when I forgot to lift my feet high enough.

The short shirt and jacket were not too different from my own clothing, at least tolerable. Maggie had brought a backpack, like the one she carried and had packed full of things, the purposes of which she hastily explained to me.

After I was dressed, she handed me some of the green papers. "Put this in your pocket. It's money."

I reviewed the marks on the papers, what she said they would mean. Folded them carefully and put them into the pocket of the pants.

Jack spoke up. "Maggie, where did you get that?"

She flushed. "It's my birthday money, some that I've saved."

I paused. "So, this money is hard to come by?"

"Umm... yeah. Most people spend their lives figuring out how to get more money, so yeah, I guess so."

How very strange. The more I learned of Maggie's world, the less comfortable I felt with our plan, but I could see no way to turn back now.

Finally, she said I was ready. Jack stood and the three of us made our way to the outskirts of the village.

"Maggie, why do you not wait here for Ash? I am sure he will be back shortly."

"Shouldn't I go with you?"

"If you don't mind, I'd rather you waited for him, then you can tell me tonight the news from my parents."

She nodded, then turned to the silent boy beside me. "Jack, aren't you going to change back before you go?"

He shrugged. "I'll change when we get to the tree. This way I can answer any more questions Bear Girl might have."

I smiled at him, grateful for his thoughtfulness.

Maggie stepped forward in a rush and hugged him. "Please be careful. Please. I know you're mad at me now——"

He interrupted. "I'm not mad and I promise, I'll be okay." He bent his head down and rested his forehead on hers. I envied them their closeness.

He broke away and started down the trail, grabbing the bag from me as he passed. "Come on, I can at least carry this for now. Who knows how much she's packed for you."

I went to Maggie and embraced her. "Thank you for all your help. And I will make sure to bring him back safely. We will see you tonight."

A weak grin crossed her face. "I know it will be all right, I'll see you soon. Good luck."

And then I turned and ran after Jack, stumbling only a little in the tight pants and awkward shoes.

I caught up with him quickly and we walked in silence, surrounded by the noise of the wind.

"Does the wind bother you?" I asked, more to have something to say than anything else.

Jack shrugged. "I hear someone crying, but after a while I can block it. I don't know if I hear it differently from the others or not."

"Jack, when you are a boy, you are a boy. Like me."

He stopped, looked at me with his eyebrows raised.

"No, not that I am a boy." I got flustered, trying to find the right words. "When I am a bear, I am a bear. Not like a normal bear, probably, but still, that is what I am. But when I wear this shape," and I ran my hands down my sides, "I am a girl, no different than anyone else in the village."

He didn't answer.

"What I am saying is that you are just as much a human boy as anyone else. You are different because you have another shape you can wear, but that is an advantage, right?"

He grinned at me. "I guess. It's hard sometimes; the only other person I can talk to about this is Coyote and he's not always the most... forthcoming with answers."

I laughed, even as I wrapped my arms around me to shield myself from the wind, missing my coat already. "Oh, I'm sure he's happy to answer questions. Just not with answers that make any sense."

We walked on, watched for the trail to bend towards the river. The closer we came, the more nervous I felt. I watched Jack, to distract myself, trying to identity the difference about him.

He spoke again and I lost my train of thought. "Are you worried about crossing?"

"What?"

"When Maggie asked what you were, I think she was worried about what might happen when you cross over. I mean," and he frowned, "is it possible, that if you're really a bear and it's just pinang that lets you wear a girl shape, will you be a bear on the other side, even without your coat?

I stopped, felt cold hands on my spine. "I... I do not know." I had feared to cross over, but had been only worried about fulfilling my task. Now I feared I would not even be able to leave. If I wore a human shape only by the grace of magic, could I wear it in a place where magic did not work?

Much too soon Jack stopped in front of a large cottonwood tree that had grown into multiple trunks, bowing away from each other, to form an upside down archway.

"Here we are."

I put the backpack on and we stood before the opening. "How are we going to do this?"

Jack grinned at me. "You need to go through first. Just wait for me after you step through. I'll be right there."

I stood before the tree, gathering my courage.

"Bear Girl, it'll be all right. I'll be right behind you."

I looked over my shoulder at him and he grinned, crazy and familiar, like a young version of Coyote—the least reassuring thing I could think of. I took a deep breath, painfully aware this would be the last breath I took of the air of my world, of my home, for a very long time.

And I stepped through the door in the tree.

The first things I noticed were the sounds. The wind did not sob and howl here, but I found no silence in its place. Low rumbles and roars came from every direction. The

66

air smelled odd, like a fire had been left burning for too long and old smoke saturated the trees. And I still wore a human shape. One question at least had been settled and some of the tightness left my chest.

I stood in place and turned to look all around me. By the heat of the air, the position of the sun and the sound of the birds I guessed it to be late afternoon. Good. We could still get much done before I needed to return with Jack to Maggie's home.

Thinking of him I turned back to the tree, impatient. Surely it could not take so long for him to rid himself of his clothing change and come through. Had something happened? Once Jack and Maggie had been trapped in my land, unable to cross back to their own. Could such a thing have happened again?

I moved towards the tree to cross back to see if he had been hurt, when out from the tree jumped... Jack.

CHAPTER EIGHT

BUT NOT THE SLEEK BLACK-AND-WHITE dog I had expected. Jack stepped through as a tall boy, wearing a grin that threatened to split his face.

He picked me up and spun me around and laughed into the faded blue sky. "It worked, it worked!"

I beat at his shoulders. "Jack, put me down!"

He twirled me twice more first.

I stared. "Jack, how did you... Did you know you could do that?"

His grin faded, but only slightly. "I've never tried it before. Coyote said it should work, that even if I can't change at home I should be able to change in your world and come back here in the other shape, but there was never time to try it and..." His smile faltered. "I was scared. I didn't know what would happen."

I nodded. "I understand. After your comment about what my true shape was, I didn't want to cross either." A thought struck me. "Does Maggie know you can do this? Or that it's even a possibility?"

He shook his head, all traces of humor gone now. "No, I never found a good time to talk to her about it." He fell silent and looked at the trees that lined the trickling irrigation ditch we stood beside.

I looked carefully at him. Away from the wind my mind felt clearer, my exhaustion lessened. I suddenly knew what had nagged me each time I had looked at Jack during this trip.

His face, formerly cubbish and plump, had grown lean. He was nearly my height. No, he was taller than I, but carried himself slouched over so as to disguise the growth.

"Jack. I have to ask you..." I thought of how to phrase this best. "How much time has passed in Maggie's world since you first came to our Land?"

He looked startled. "Almost a year, why?"

I studied his face, his form. "I do not think you are only a year older. You look to be close to my own age now. Before, when you first changed, you were younger than Maggie; now I think you are her age, or older."

Jack reared back as if I had attacked him. "Can we talk about this later? I don't think it's going to help us any."

I agreed reluctantly. Once I had solved the mystery of the wind and felt secure that my parents and the rest of our people were safe, I would turn my attention to what troubled Jack.

"Jack, what are we going to do about your clothing?"

He looked down at the buckskins which had been so appropriate in the village, but I was sure would be out of place here.

He frowned briefly, then took the backpack from me. "Knowing Maggie she packed you extra, right? I'll just borrow those." He fished out another pair of the blue pants and a long-sleeved overshirt.

"I'll just go change, be right back." He walked back through the cottonwood and I shuddered. What if something happened this time? I stopped myself. It was luckier than I could imagine that Jack would be able to help me in his boy form. I should stop worrying over every detail.

Jack came back, still wearing the buckskin pants but with the new shirt. "Jeans don't fit at all. Shirt's a little tight, but it'll do. And I'm not sure what we'll do about shoes. Maybe no one will notice?"

I looked at his feet. "I will give you these. I do not know how anyone can stay in these."

He looked down. "Um, no. Those are girl shoes."

I looked again. They were pink with red trim and tied loosely to my feet. I shrugged. "As you prefer. So, how does this change our plans?"

"It's a million times better! First off, we can take the bus to the University. That'll save a ton of time and be cheaper than the taxi, too."

Something moved behind me and Jack rushed forward. "Ducks!"

Jack stood on the edge of the bank, nose twitching, leaning forward at a steep incline.

"Jack, be careful!"

"It's all different. Doesn't smell the same, but it's still home." He ran back and forth up the path, pointing out trees and fences and other dogs.

"Hi, Bouncer! Hi, Duchess! It's me, it's me!"

A large tan dog with a whip-like tail stood before the fence, her head cocked to the side. Jack stood before the fence separating them and she advanced and sniffed the air.

Just as I began to worry that his friends would no longer recognize him her tail wagged furiously. She leapt and spun in circles.

"I know, isn't it great?" He looked over his shoulder at me. "I wonder if I can teach the others how to change too!"

I laughed, then caught myself. What if he could? And then what would that do? Would it create a whole city of dogs who were tired and bored with their lives? Would they all leave, demand to go to the school that occupied Maggie's time?

"I am sure you can teach them all. But later, please!" I took a hold of his arm and continued walking down the trail. "It is this way, yes?"

"You're right." But he looked over his shoulder at Duchess and paused for brief hellos when he saw his other friends as we passed. I did not stop him.

71

We left the trail after a while and descended a short hill down to a hard black surface lined with buildings that stood one or two stories high, with doors and large windows on the lower floors as well as the upper ones. Little pieces of land surrounded each, but not nearly enough for a garden. I looked at Jack, confused.

"Most houses are stand-alone buildings here," he explained. "Sort of like your parents', but, well, not in the side of a cliff."

I nodded and made a decision; I would treat all of this world as a dream, an illusion, in which anything was possible and do my best to look to Jack for clues. If he acted like all was normal, like nothing was out of the ordinary, I would do the same.

Jack kept looking at one of the strange houses in particular.

"Jack, what is wrong? Is there a problem with that house?"

He shrugged. "That's my house. Mine and Maggie's house. Mom and Dad aren't there right now, but I feel like I should go home, go inside and wait. It's stranger than anything I could imagine, that I could walk in, fix myself a sandwich, actually say hello to our parents." He looked sad. "I wonder what they would say."

I put my arm around his waist and hugged him while we walked past the long adobe building with the curved wall in the front, the gesture made awkward by the backpack Jack wore.

"I'm sure they would love you, no matter what shape you wore. You and Maggie love them very much and I am sure you could not if they were not good people, true?"

He nodded, but I could see in his eyes he was not convinced.

"Come on, show me this thing called a bus."

We stopped by a low gray bench. "This should take us there. This is the stop I've seen when we're walking."

He pointed to a metal square on a pole by the bench. "And that number is the same Maggie told you about, the same on the bus map. All right, you'll need to get the money ready."

I reached back into my pocket and pulled out the slips of green paper.

"Bear Girl, do you want me to hold those? I see Maggie use them all the time."

I nodded, happy to have one less thing to worry about.

He stared at them intently, then pulled one of the papers out of the stack. "This should work."

We waited until the bus came, a thing like a house that moved, rumbling and bouncing down the road. It stopped before us and a section of the wall slid open.

We both stared at it. I did not know what to do and I think being in this shape here, doing all the things that were forbidden, still overwhelmed Jack.

A short run of stairs led up to a woman with short frizzy hair.

"Get on if you're coming, kids! I have a schedule to keep."

I put my hand on the silver rail and mounted the stairs with Jack pressed behind me.

The seat directly behind the woman was empty and I sank into it, staring out the window.

Bus Woman spoke to Jack. "No, kid. You need exact change."

He stood at the front of the bus, holding out the slip of paper to her.

"That's a five, you need to put in two ones." She pointed to a tall box that stood next to her. Jack looked confused and flustered.

I hurried back over to him and took the pile of other papers out of his hand and shuffled through them. I found two with the markings Maggie had shown me as "ones" and handed them to the woman.

73

She made an exasperated noise and slid them into a slot on the tall box. "If you're exchange students, you should have someone with you. Don't know why you don't."

I grabbed Jack's arm and sat down behind the woman again.

"I am sorry. I am new here. This will take us to the," I fought for the strange words, "The University area, yes?"

She laughed. "Don't worry about it, hon, this won't be the worst thing that happens to me today." She did something with her hands and the door closed and the large box moved down the street. "And yeah," she continued. "This will get you to the campus."

I blinked and Jack whispered. "Campus is the University. Same thing."

Why could she not have said that?

Before long, I had more than enough things to push the behavior of Bus Woman out of my mind. The bus moved through many trails, stopped at intervals to let people on and off, then kept traveling. I tried to estimate how far we had gone and could not. Everywhere I looked, more people, more buildings, more cars swarmed around us. I felt woozy.

"Hey, are you getting car sick?" Jack whispered.

"I do not know what that is, but I do not feel well."

He took my hand. "We're almost there, it'll be okay. Um, one of Maggie's friends gets carsick and she always says that looking out at something far away that doesn't move helps. Look at the mountains and I'll watch for where we get off."

At the edge of the city, mountains rose to the sky; their tops covered with snow. In my overwhelmed state I had not noticed them and now I clung to their image. "Jack, what direction is that?" It did not matter, but I wanted to have at least one thing that made sense to me in this strange place.

"The mountains are to the east of the city. Maggie uses

them as reference when we're out exploring."

East. Knowing that was a start.

Shortly Jack squeezed my hand. "We're almost there, time to get off."

The bus rolled to a stop and many of the riders stood. We waited in line, pressed far too close to people I had never met.

I waited while Jack turned in place slowly.

"I need to see where we are. Usually when we come down, Mom or Dad drives us and we park somewhere else. But I'm sure I'll figure out a landmark soon."

He took my hand and pulled me along behind him.

"Come on, let's get onto campus. I'll see something I recognize."

"Or we can ask someone," I said. But I did not think he heard me.

We walked up a set of broad steps with large buildings to either side that stood almost as large as my home cliff. I wondered about what sort of people could build such a thing.

In a moment we stood by a large, brightly colored statue of a man and a woman.

Jack looked at it and nodded. "Okay, I know where we are!" We headed to the left away from the statue, then down a narrow passageway formed by two buildings pressed closely to each other.

Before us stood a strange gray shape. Jack laughed. "The Center of the Universe! You've got to see this." And he pulled me after him.

We walked around the thing. Large, made of smooth slabs of gray stone, as if someone had taken four rooms and arranged them so they stuck out to each of the directions and then another block on the top.

"Come on, it makes more sense inside."

We walked inside the thing. Each of the sides stood open, forming tunnels that allowed you to see through the odd building in each of the four directions.

"Look up."

The block on top was open as well, a short tunnel leading to the sky.

"Look down."

We stood on a woven piece of metal, over a sixth open cube.

"See?" Jack asked. "It's the center of the universe. If you stand in the middle, it goes all around you."

I nodded. This was the first thing that had made sense to me, something that marked the six directions. I stood there for a moment, regaining my own center.

"Thank you for showing this to me."

Jack smiled eyes bright with happiness. I liked seeing him that way, rather than troubled as he had been for so much of the last day.

He tugged my hand. "We're right by the duck pond. Let's go see if we can find out what Spider Old Woman thinks you'll learn there."

Jack led me up a short grassy hill and at the top we looked down.

This was it. The grass sloping down to the water. A pond with a small island. Ducks swam by. A cluster of trees to one side with a rock jutting out into the water. People lying on the grass, sitting, reading books. This was the exact place of my vision.

I turned and hugged Jack. "You were right!"

He looked flustered. "What? You didn't trust me?"

I rolled my eyes. "Of course. But I'm still happy we found the right place so quickly. With this sort of luck on our side, I am sure we can find the source of the wind, fix the problem and both of us go home."

He ran a hand through his shaggy hair and grinned. "Well, as long as you're happy."

"Let us continue to search and see if we can find the next step."

We walked around the very edge of the pond, but found nothing but children and ducks and people feeding them. The brown water looked filthy, but the ducks did not mind.

We found nothing that warranted further exploration and so spiraled outward, circling the pond, slowly making our way to the outer paved area.

And then we found him, the young man from my vision. He ran a hand through his light hair, shoving it from his face as he hurried by.

I grabbed Jack's arm to follow, but he pulled me back. "It's Dad! Quick, we have to hide!"

"Him?" I pointed to the young man. He did not look much older than us, certainly not old enough to be Maggie's father.

"No, over there." And he pointed in the direction the young man ran.

An older man walked towards us, with glasses and a coat. Tall and thin, I could see traces of Maggie in his walk and I wondered if she knew she looked like her father when she was lost in thought.

The younger man ran after him, calling "Professor Sanger! Professor Sanger!"

"Let's follow them."

"What? No!" Jack's face was pale. "He can't see me out, not like this!"

"How many people does your father know who can change their shape?"

Jack looked at me, startled. "Um, none. People don't do that here."

"Then how could he ever suspect that you are you?"

We followed them to where Maggie's father waited for the younger man with a look of impatience.

"Sorry, Dr. Sanger, I just didn't get down what time we're meeting tomorrow."

Maggie's father rolled his eyes. "If you'd been listening, you'd have known. 2 p.m. If you're bringing your family, make sure they meet the buses at the Wilson building."

The young man nodded, a little flushed. "Thanks, I know they can't wait to see the new dig."

The two men entered one of the buildings and I felt uncomfortable following further. I turned to Jack. "We should go talk with Maggie, and find out what your father has been doing. He must be our next clue."

CHAPTER NINE

ARLY EVENING SHADOWS STRETCHED OVER the road by the time we reached the park by Maggie's house. Our stomachs reminded us we had not eaten since we left the village that morning. Jack led me to an area of grass and stone benches, deserted in the fading light.

He set the backpack down on a park bench. "If I know Maggie..." and he rummaged through the pack.

"I knew it!" he crowed, holding up two wrapped packages.

"What are these?"

He laughed. "Cheese sandwiches. Maggie doesn't go anywhere without them. They're great." He looked through the pack again, found another. "Let's go ahead and have them all. I don't usually have more than one, but today I might."

I smiled and thought of all the times I had seen her share her sandwich with her constant companion. The smile faded as I wondered what this expedition would mean for the two of them.

We ate in silence and Jack showed me a rock fountain that could be controlled with a lever for us to drink out of. Very useful, but very strange, like most of this place.

As we ate I stumbled for words. "This morning, you asked me to wait before talking to you about something. And I have. But we are going to see Maggie soon and before we go, I need to have all the information I can."

He turned his face to me, his eyes sad. "I don't want to talk about it."

"Jack, do you think it would be easier to talk to me about this, or to Maggie? At some point, she is going to notice something is different, something has changed. I think she is already starting to notice." I put my hand over his. "I am your friend. I will help you find a way to tell her. But you must explain to me what is happening."

He wrapped his fingers around mine and stared into the sun as it lowered to the horizon. The sky became streaked with vivid orange and reds.

Perhaps I had pushed too hard. "Even the sunset is different here. Brighter, more colors."

Jack smiled weakly. "Dad says that's because of the pollutants, um, like the smoke that the cars and factories put out into the air. The light hits those in the air and makes the sunsets more brilliant. It's a pretty thing, but may kill us in the end." He squeezed my hand. "I think I'm dying."

I blurted the first principle of my training: "All mortal things die. It is their nature." I spoke hurriedly to soften my words. "Are you sick? What can I do?"

He shrugged. "I'm not sick. I think you're right, actually. This is in my nature." He turned his face to me. Tears stood in his eyes. "I know things are different between our worlds, but here... here animals do not live as long as people. They say every year of a dog's life is like seven human years."

I thought about this, inspected it in my mind, found the issue he had not addressed. "What does Maggie say about this?"

"She doesn't know yet. I don't want her to know."

"How can she not know, if this is common knowledge? How can she not know just to look at you?"

He looked back at the darkening sky. "A part of her must know. But I don't want her to think about it. I don't want to think about it. We've never been apart and this means I'll be gone, long before Maggie and we'll be separated forever."

I could say nothing in the face of this truth, but sit next to him and rest my head on his shoulder. We watched the day end together.

Jack judged it time for us to head to Maggie's house to check in. He had wanted to wait until after her family had eaten, when Maggie would be in her room working on homework.

As we walked we talked about where I should stay for the night.

"Go home, then come back in the morning." Jack decreed. "It'd be safer there, even with the wind."

"I do not want to lose so much time. It is possible that the difference in time would aid me, but I cannot count on that. I need to stay here until this puzzle is solved." I considered options. "I will return to where we ate the sandwiches and sleep there. There are bushes and few people. It will be comfortable enough."

Jack halted. "No way! You can't go sleep in a park. It's too cold to sleep outside and besides, it's not safe."

"Jack, how much safer can I be? I am a bear, after all."

He shook his head. "Not here, you're not. No sleeping in parks."

We had not resolved the issue when we arrived at Maggie's house. Jack led us around the side, through a gate and towards a window at the back. We crouched low, inching our way along. Then Jack stiffened, his eyes wide as a man spoke. The voice we'd heard this afternoon at the school sounded as if it came from directly above us.

"I just don't know, honey. We'll have to wait and see what happens."

A woman answered. "I never thought this would happen. Do you think someone could have taken him?"

The man's reply was muffled as we crawled away.

We stopped beneath a far window and Jack reached up and scratched the glass. Within seconds the pane slid to the side and Maggie stood in front of us.

"Come in, come in, quiet!"

We crawled over the windowsill into her room and crouched down behind her bed. The door that I supposed led to the rest of the house was on the other side of the room, so that if her parents came in they would see nothing. We hoped.

I remained silent while Maggie and Jack stared at each other. She glared at him, outrage stamped across her features. "You're still a boy?" Her soft question carried hurt with it. "Why didn't you tell me you were going to be like this?"

He reached forwards, then stopped his hand as she pulled back. "I didn't know if I could do it, didn't know if I could keep the change here. I would have told you if I knew for sure."

Her eyebrows drawn together, Maggie shook her head. "I would have packed tons better if I'd known." She bit her lip, as if to stop herself from arguing. "But what did you find out?"

Stumbling over each other, we told her about finding the young man of my vision, and how he had led us to her father.

"We still do not know what is causing the wind. It may be a false trail, but his appearance may provide the next clue."

Maggie nodded slowly. "He's been busy lately with a dig."

"The other man said that, but I am not sure what he meant."

Maggie explained. "An archeological dig. Where they find things that have been lost, or buried under the dust, or sometimes under newer buildings while they're being built. Around here people used to find old abandoned pueblos, or old houses, or sometimes graves."

I shook my head. "I think it would have to be something

new, for it to affect my home so suddenly. Time moves differently between our worlds, but I cannot believe that we would just now be seeing the effects of something that happened so long ago here!"

Jack spoke up. "Maybe they found something old, but just recently." He shrugged. "It's the only thing that makes sense. If any of this does."

"He's taking a lot of students and their families to the dig site tomorrow," Maggie said. "Maybe you could try to follow?"

"Maybe we can just go with them. I'd bet people would just assume we're someone else's kids. Just meet with everyone else in the afternoon, and we're good to go."

I looked closely at Jack. He'd clearly been spending too much time with Coyote, but I could not argue with his plan.

"Then we will wait for tomorrow. I wish we did not have to wait so long." My voice trailed off and I thought of my parents, the new lines on my mother's face, the weariness in my father's step and bowed my head.

Maggie touched my arm softly. "I did wait for Ash."

My throat tightened. "What did he find?"

"Your parents are all right. Tired, but hanging in there."

A shadow lay on her words. "What else is wrong?"

"I think Ash is getting sick. A lot of people who were fine before are so tired now. It's like the wind is wearing them down."

I hugged her. "I'll do my best to stop it, as soon as I can."

She nodded, leaned back against the high-padded bed and closed her eyes.

"Maggie," Jack's voice was nearly inaudible. "What did you tell Mom and Dad?"

She did not answer him for a moment and when she did the bitterness in her voice struck me. "What did you think I told them? They don't know how it could have happened and they think I left the gate unlatched. There's no other way for you to have gotten out."

His face tightened and I wanted to tell her not to be cruel, but this lay between them and it was not my place, no matter how I felt.

She took a deep breath. "I'm sorry. I hate having to act like I wouldn't have been careful about you." She gave a pale excuse for a smile. "Besides, I keep having to pretend to cry and we both know I'm a lousy actress."

He looked at her and tried a smile back of his own and they touched for the first time since we had crawled through the window.

Maggie wiped away a tear. "Jack, you're going to have to pay for this, you know." She sounded as if she tried to keep her voice light, but I could hear her distress. "We spent an hour or so before dinner putting up lost dog signs. You're pretty safe in that shape though; no one will report finding you."

She pushed the topic away. "Have you decided what you're going to do tonight?"

"Yes," he answered.

"No," I shot.

Jack and I glared at each other.

"Yes," he continued. "Bear Girl is going to go back home for the night and then start again."

"No, I'm not," I insisted.

Maggie looked at us. "Wow. I can only imagine what your day must have been like. I think I have an answer for you if you can stand it."

We stopped glaring at each other and looked at her.

"There's a house under construction a block over. They don't have all the doors up, yet. I'd bet you could stay there and as long as you were up early enough, no one would even know. Jack, it's almost right behind Mrs. Bishop's place. Think you could find it?"

Jack grinned. "Mrs. Bishop gives me treats every time

we see her. Yeah, I can find the street behind her house, no problem."

Maggie looked at me. "Would this work for you?"

I felt uneasy. "Is this not someone else's home? I do not think I am comfortable taking someone's house."

Maggie shook her head. "There's no one living there now. It would be like... like..."

Jack cut in. "Like sleeping in an abandoned nest. You're not kicking out the bird who built it, she's not there any more, doesn't care."

I looked at him, looked at them both. "If you say so. I am still uncertain." But I did not know what else to do.

Maggie made sure we knew where the meeting place for the bus would be, and found a pair of thin sandals for Jack and handed him a light blanket from the foot of her bed.

"I don't know how warm it'll be tonight. If you're not going to be home, at least take this with you."

Jack sniffed the blanket and smiled. I caught the scent of Jack the dog. He must have used it often in his other shape.

We hugged Maggie then climbed out her window and crawled back around the house and to the street. Jack found the house with no trouble. It stood with the fragments of light from the surrounding houses shining through the empty upper levels. We stood under the tree of the house across the street and watched it. There was no one to be seen, no movement; it was entirely dark and abandoned.

Jack found a large hole in the back wall that must have been waiting for a door to be put into place. Now only a flap of thick gray material hung down, reminding me of deer skins covering the doors of the rooms in Ash's village.

We pushed our way in and crept through the house. Room opened into room, ceilings arched high over our heads.

"Jack," I whispered and when he did not stop, I reached

forward to touch his shoulder. He jumped and glared at me, but I knew he listened to me now.

"How many families will live here when this house is completed?" I could imagine it filled with men and women, children spilling down the stairways, halls echoing with laughter.

He looked confused. "Probably just one, why?"

"One? Then, do they have many children? Will the aunts and uncles and grandparents live here as well?"

He looked around, appeared to search for traces of something. "Um, no. Probably not. Two or three kids at most."

All of this, for only five people and three of them children? I shook my head, gave up worrying about it and focused on Jack as he resumed his trek through the house.

We found a room near the middle of the house, with no windows to betray us to the outside world.

"Just in case," Jack said.

We cleared a space on the floor and sat. A light chill enveloped the house, not terribly cold, but enough that I wished for the comfort of my coat and was glad for the blanket. I looked at Jack and wondered.

"Wish you could change for sleeping?"

He stopped patting the ground around himself. "Yeah, I guess I do. I haven't actually slept in this shape very often. I can't curl up the way I want."

After a time of tossing and turning, arranging and fidgeting, we settled in.

"Bear Girl," he whispered. "Why do you keep saying you don't have magic?" He went on, unaware of my clenched fists. "These dreams, or visions, or whatever, are coming and finding you. And just you. From what you said, even Spider Old Woman wanted to see them through your eyes."

"Jack, I do not want to talk about this. Not tonight, not ever. I am a healer, I am the daughter of healers and whatever is happening, I do not want this."

"But—"

"No."

I rolled away from him and after time I heard Jack's breathing slow down, become steady and deep.

I stared at the ceiling, dreading a night filled with worry and wakefulness, but the day's exhaustion, after so many days of treating the sick at the village, took its toll and I felt myself dragged down into sleep.

"Isabel, I need to talk to you."

The piebald sheep turned their faces towards Tomás as he approached.

"I will be finished soon."

He took the bucket away from Isabel and scattered the grain wildly.

"Tomás!" She threw her arms up. "How can you be done in the fields already? You have your work to do as well."

He shrugged. "That is not important right now. Right now I need to speak to you."

"Tomás, stop." She reached forward, grabbed his arm, halted his movement. "If I leave my chores, I'll be scolded." She laughed. "If Fray Alonzo even notices." Her face sobered. "But if you are missing, he can have you flogged. I do not want that."

Tomás nodded. "I promise. He will not notice. I have made sure my work is done. And now," with a final shake of the grain pail, "your work is done too."

They twisted through the streets until they reached the middle of the new town, the tall building of the mission in front of them, the wooden doors carved with stars and flowers.

Tomás led her around the edge of the building to the narrow side door. He pushed it open a crack, looked around, then slipped inside, pulling her behind him.

"What are you—"

His hand over her mouth cut off her whisper. Her dark eyes widened as he bent his face down to hers.

"You must be silent now, I will explain all later," he hissed.

She nodded, face white, eyes fixed on his.

He uncovered her mouth, then moved away to kneel in the corner. Isabel crept closer, watched him work at the seam between two pieces of flagstone with a thin blade.

"What—"

His sharp look silenced her and he continued working while she bit her fingers.

Within moments the stone was free and he lifted it and set it to the side. He reached into the hole and came out with a handheld lantern. He lit it and the faint glow revealed a ladder stretching down into the blackness.

"Come on." He sat on the edge of the hole and held the lantern out.

Isabel shook her head. "No." Her lips formed the word, but no sound came out.

"Isabel, it is safe. Come down."

The girl shook, arms crossed over her chest. "I don't want to go down there with the snakes and spiders."

"There are no..." He sighed. "If I go first, will you follow?"

She nodded.

"Really?"

She glared at him. "I have never lied to you before; I am not about to start doing so now."

He climbed down the ladder, taking the lantern with him.

The room darkened as the lantern descended and she crept closer to the hole and the light. Within moments his voice came from the pit.

"It is all right. No snakes, no spiders."

She gathered her skirts around her legs and sat on the edge of the pit. She felt around for the ladder, then lowered herself into the hole.

"Tomás!" she hissed.

"What now?"

"Don't look up!"

He sighed.

The walls of the pit were formed of stacked stone. The bottom was packed earth, hardened with ox blood. The width of the chamber would easily surpass thirty paces. This was not a random hole in the ground, but a room, built deep into the earth.

"What is this place?"

Tomás shook his head and looked sad. "You are one of us, your mother was one of our people, but they took you away, took you from your heritage."

She glared at him. "I have heard this and heard this since I have been back to the pueblo. My family has taken me from nothing."

"Then how can you not know the kiva, the sacred space, sacred even though they build their buildings over it?"

She spat the words, "My mother was a Christian, the same as me, the same as you and the people of the village, Spanish or Indian. You took their oaths, you come to Mass."

Tomás put the lantern on the floor, let its light cast their shadows on the walls where they flickered with agitation. "Yes, some of us believe truly. Your mother was one. She converted, she married one of the invaders, she left her home and people, she told you nothing of your true people.

"But most of us do as they tell us because we have no choice. If we do not convert, if we do not work in their fields, then we have nothing to live on. Once we held our own lands, our own fields. Now the Spanish hold everything. They took our land, raided the grain we had stored. We have nothing to trade with the other villages, nothing to keep us through lean years, nothing at all now."

He looked up at her, face wild.

"And our people can take no more."

Isabel shook her head. "Why do you tell me this? What do you want me to do?"

"You must go, you must leave here."

She staggered back as if he had struck her. "What? You want me to leave?"

He came towards her, held his hands out to her shoulders, but she backed away.

"I thought you were waiting for my father to return. I thought, I thought..." She backed into the wall, could go no further.

"Shhhh." He held her arms. "I do not want you to go. But I think you should. I want you to go, to tell Fray Alonzo to go with you, to return to Santa Fe and if you can, to go south."

She shook her head. "But this is my home. If I leave, how will my father find me?"

His hands closed on her arms, pressing through the thin fabric, shaking her.

"None of that matters now. You must leave here, leave here as soon as you can."

She spun away from him and kicked over the lantern, dropping the kiva into velvet blackness.

<hr>

I woke up, choking. I could feel the marks on my arm where the boy had squeezed her, had shaken her.

"Bear Girl, what is it?"

Jack shot up next to me and looked around the room for danger.

"A dream, the people from the vision. Something's terribly wrong. Whatever it is, it's getting worse, getting closer."

Jack lay back down. "Whatever it is, I don't think we're going to figure it out tonight."

He reached up and pulled me down until I lay against his chest. He wrapped his arms tightly around me and stroked my hair. "You sleep and I'll watch for a while. Just have normal dreams, okay?"

I smiled. I did not want to see further into their world and I did not think that Jack would be able to stop it. But it was nice that he would be willing to try. Sooner than I expected I drifted into dreamless sleep.

CHAPTER TEN

THE FIRST LIGHT OF MORNING filtered in from the outer rooms and I untangled myself from Jack. I stretched, missing all the comforts of being home. Mother. Father. My throat caught. No. No time.

"Jack," I reached out and shook him. "Come on, we need to leave."

Asleep, I could see traces of the younger boy he had been, but as he woke the years fell into place.

"Morning." He stood, stretched. "Breakfast. Let's get some breakfast."

We started down the road.

"Where can we cook breakfast here?"

He grinned. "You're going to love this. Heck, I'm going to love this. I've never gotten to go inside before."

We went to a compact building with people streaming in and out the doors. Cars in a line wrapped around the building.

"What is this?" I whispered.

"A restaurant. They have a window they hand food out of. Dad takes us for breakfast burritos here sometimes on the weekends. Maggie gets the really big one so we can split it. Sometimes if the line is long she goes inside instead, but I have to wait in the car. Now I don't!"

I blinked. "You know, the only words of that I understood were breakfast and Maggie."

He shrugged. "Sorry. But I know you'll like it."

We waited in line, amid a press of people dressed in all

sorts of different ways. Women in skirts or in pants, men in long pants or short pants, woven of every color I could think of. The line shuffled forward and we eventually arrived at the front.

"Two number ones, please, red."

Red? I wondered.

Jack held out a stack of the green papers from Maggie and the woman at the high table took some, gave him different papers back, then handed him a bag and turned her attention to the people behind us.

We sat at a small table outside. "Jack, what just happened?"

"We bought breakfast. I told you that was a restaurant."

"You can pay people to cook for you?" I thought about that, about all the mornings I had struggled to prepare food despite being half asleep. "So, you just give them money and they give you... what is this?"

Jack had handed me a thick roll of flat bread wrapped around steaming contents. He busily ate his own. "Mmmph mmmh."

"That does not help." But I took the bundle and nibbled at the corner of the bundle.

"Mmmm!" Warm spicy food filled the roll and a red sauce spilled out over my hand.

"Good, isn't it? Eggs, potatoes, other stuff and this spicy red sauce. Best breakfast ever."

I kept eating and wondered how I could make something like this at home.

We finished and licked the last of the sauce off our fingers, laughing.

"I want to have someone cook for me all the time!" I declared.

Jack shook his head. "We can only do it for a few days. Every time it takes some of the money from Maggie and in a while we'll run out." He looked up at me and I felt myself answer his smile. "But that won't happen for a while yet, so no worries!"

Breakfast was the only good part of the morning. It felt like the time for us to meet the buses would never come. We went back to the campus, to the place Maggie had told us was the building that the young man had mentioned. I drove Jack crazy, worrying if we were on the right trail, if I should be doing something else.

Finally several buses arrived, painted differently from the ones we had already ridden. They parked in a line, and shortly after their arrival groups of people drifted in from all directions.

"Those must be the families of the students," Jack whispered. "Dad tries to make sure there's some sort of field trip for everyone at least once a year. He says if the whole family is interested, the students do better in school."

I grunted, only giving him half my attention. Maggie's father stood by the opening to the bus at the front of the line, so I pulled Jack towards one of the others, where we waited near several families. Jack's plan worked. No one questioned us and soon we boarded the bus and were on the way.

After we had taken a seat near the back a thought struck me. "Get out the map," I whispered. "Let us see if we can trace where we are going."

The bus twisted through narrow streets for a few minutes, but shortly entered a larger street and went straight.

"We're going south, I think," whispered Jack. He glanced over at the mountains to be sure.

After a few minutes, a young woman at the front of the bus stood up and spoke to the rest of the passengers.

"Dr. Sanger would like to make sure that everyone has a little background on where we're going. Since I'm one of his students, that would be my job. Let me know if you have any questions. Spanish explorers first came into the territory now known as New Mexico in 1532 and quickly spread the belief that rich treasures of gold and silver would be found here, just as they had been in New Spain, what we call Mexico, to the South.

"In 1610 Santa Fe became the new capital. Caravans of colonists made the six-month journey north from New Spain. They brought cattle and sheep and the knowledge of forging metal.

"They also brought their religion. The Spanish king, disappointed by the lack of treasure, considered abandoning the colony. But Franciscan missionaries had traveled through the region and they argued that it was needful to keep a Christian presence.

"Villages that fought the Spanish faced severe punishment. The Spanish soldiers, poorly provisioned, demanded the villages turn over their stores of grain. When years of drought came, the Pueblo people had no choice but to move closer to the invaders and accept the new ways.

"The land itself contributed to the hardship. The Rio Grande valley went through several years of drought. Years of drought and famine, as well as the forced service of the Pueblo people to the Spanish and repression of the native religion raised tensions to unbearable heights.

"In 1680 those tensions boiled over. In August of that year, Pueblo warriors throughout New Mexico united, despite barriers of culture and language that had historically kept the Pueblos separate.

"They burned the churches and killed many of the priests and settlers. The warriors then surrounded Santa Fe where many of the surviving settlers had taken refuge. After they cut off the water supply to the town, the governor Antonio de Otermín was forced to retreat. A thousand Spanish settlers fled to Mexico."

Otermín. I had heard that name in my vision. We were on the right trail, after all.

"The Spanish returned to reclaim the territory twelve

years later, but this was the first and last time that a
European force would be removed from a colony in North
America until the American war of revolution. What you're
going to see today is a truly interesting part of this story."

Her voice had not changed once, not throughout her
tale of suffering and horror. I could not imagine what she
would think was interesting.

"Twenty years ago, the owner of some property in the
South Valley cleared land to put up a new barn. Under
the brush she discovered the remains of a previously
undiscovered pueblo and mission. It must have been
deserted after the revolt. We found the pueblo was called
Santa Catalina. Having an untouched pueblo within a city
is a great opportunity for research. A month ago, we had
a fantastic discovery."

My ears pricked up. A month. How long would that be
at home?

"One of the student teams tested a new piece of
equipment that uses sonar to look for things buried under
the ground."

A woman in front of us raised her hand, and the young
woman paused.

"Sonar takes sound waves and pushes them through
the ground until the sound waves hit something dense
enough to bounce back and then the machine can see a
sketchy picture of what's down there. Almost like how a
bat 'sees' in the dark."

I kept my face still. I wanted to yell that this did not
help, but I supposed I had enough of the idea for her
to continue.

"They found that the mission had been built over
the old kiva, an underground room where pueblo people
performed sacred rituals. Actually, a lot of the missions
were built that way."

"The sonar also found two bodies, not terribly well
preserved, tangled together down at the bottom of the

kiva. That was pretty unexpected. We don't know how they died, or who they were, or what they were doing there. Our people had to separate them to get them out and now Dr. Sanger is leading a team running tests back at the University."

Bodies. Bodies disturbed after all this time. I thought of the pit Tomás had brought Isabel into. I wondered if she had ever come out of that dark place.

The buses pulled into a dirt lot filled with other cars. I did not wait for Jack before leaving the bus, but flung myself towards a wooden bench and pulled my knees up to my chest, wrapped my arms around them as tightly as I could. Nothing warmed me. The sun's light was far away and I shook, thinking of the horrors the woman's voice had so calmly described.

I heard someone approach from behind and Jack crouched next to me.

"Bear Girl?" He said nothing else, but I heard the question in his voice.

I shook my head. "I do not blame them. I do not blame the Spanish. In the span of days, I am sure all parties did only what they thought was needful. But," I stopped, searched for words, for an explanation of the revulsion that shook through me. "My family, they are healers. We always have been. We always will be. That is what I am trained for."

Jack nodded, looked unsure as to where my words led.

"For a healer, to hear of all those deaths, all of that anger, from both sides, the cruelty and the pain... and to know there is nothing to be done, nothing that could have been done, even if I had been there. It breaks my heart."

He said nothing, but put an arm around me and I felt the warmth of his body sink into mine as I leaned back against his chest.

I could hear him hum softly as he thought. "But... I don't understand something. How did you not know about this? Isn't it part of the past? Something you would know?"

I squirmed in his embrace to face him. "What do you mean?"

His brow furrowed and I could tell he was trying to put his words together. "Where you and Ash come from. I guess I always thought it was somewhere in the past, somewhere in history. So I figured you would know this stuff, about when the Spanish came and all that."

"I do not think it works like that." I settled back and watched people flow around us. "The more time I spend here, the more time I have spoken with you and Maggie, the more I think there is something different between your world and mine. There is always Spider Old Woman and Coyote. Always our people. We have stories, tales of long ago, but our present does not seem to change as rapidly as your world."

"What about last summer? The evil old guy just about wiped out Ash's village. That doesn't sound unchanging to me."

I shook my head. "I had not forgotten. Ripples come and go, people change. Perhaps a new village will arise and an old one vanishes." I bit my lip, remembering old tales. "We do have stories of people leaving, of them wandering away, looking for a different home. They never return and no one hears from them."

Jack grunted. "Huh. I wonder if maybe they came here. I know Maggie found stories about Spider Old Woman and Coyote in local folk tales. Maybe people from your world came here, started villages." He sat up, excited. "Maybe the people here are your descendants, or part of your family. Long-lost cousins!"

I laughed at him. "I don't think so. Maybe they are related to Ash and his people, but I doubt they are from my family. Unless there are families of talking bears."

"No..." he laughed with me and I felt better.

"So, do you think you found answers to what you were

looking for?"

I straightened. "We must find out more."

Jack tightened his arm around my shoulders. "When you're ready, we'll go on."

The other visitors wandered through, glancing about the dig. I wondered if they felt the weight of the ruin, as if someone had erased everything but the last few bricks of a city. Only the outlines of the buildings remained. Time and wind and rain had worn the adobe down, so that no wall stood taller than my knees. Grass and weeds grew up through what once had been hard-packed floors. I guessed the gardens that once supported the pueblo lay underneath the modern looking house some distance to the right.

Jack squeezed my hand. "Let's look around a little."

Bright-orange strips of fabric marked off the ruins of the buildings. The other visitors stood by each one, looked around, moved on. I do not know what they sought to find in such a place. An empty village, so long gone that even the stones did not remain. My mouth tasted of ashes.

Maggie's father spoke to a group of people, and while I did not think he posed a danger to us, being near him made Jack uncomfortable. We stayed at the edges of the group. From there we were able to see something we had missed coming in.

A man addressed a cluster of people gathered outside the gate. Even from a distance I could see some strong emotion twisted his face. "Let's go see what he's saying." I wandered closer.

"Every day we wait, and every day we are told to wait more. What we ask for is only right and decent. This is not a place that should be examined by scientists and students, but to be returned to us for care. It is our right." He continued, but I could not hear more over the other noise. I stepped closer and into the path of the young woman who had spoken to our group on the bus.

"He's here again." She didn't sound surprised. "Don't let him bother you kids, ok?"

Jack spoke up first. "We're not worried, but what is he talking about?"

She blew her hair out of her face. "Most of the Pueblo people understand what we're doing here. We're not grave robbers. There are all sorts of rules about this, and Dr. Sanger makes sure we follow them. The skeletons will be returned to the Pueblo Council for reburial as soon as they are examined. But some people aren't happy that we're involved at all. There's a group that wants the University to stop investigating right now and just go away. Luckily it's not very many people."

I looked again at the speaker. Although his group nodded and muttered in agreement, they were few, only five or six.

"Don't let them rattle you," she finished, and was caught up in another conversation with an older man and woman.

Jack caught my hand and whispered. "Bear Girl, look over there."

I forced my attention to where Jack pointed. Nothing but another ruin, larger perhaps, with more strips sealing it away from unwary feet. A sign stood in front of it, no doubt explaining what the building was, but such a thing did us no good. I looked, but saw nothing unusual. "Jack, what am I looking for?"

He flicked a glance over to me. Frowned. "You don't see her?"

I looked again. No one stood by the building.

"No, I don't see anyone."

"Ah. Well, that explains it then."

Some times he could be truly maddening. "Explains what?"

He sighed. "I see a girl, running back and forth in long skirts that might be faded blue, or gray. And a white blouse with patterns stitched into it."

"Embroidery," I murmured, staring at the empty ground that had caught his attention.

"Her hair is long and dark, almost as dark as yours, and she has it in two braids that hang down her back. Her skin is golden, but paler. Not nearly as pale as Maggie, though." He looked at me again. "I think maybe she's a ghost."

I nodded. "I think you are right, for you have perfectly described the girl in my visions." I stared at him, stricken. "How can you see her?"

Jack laughed. "Because I'm a dog, remember? Everyone knows dogs can see ghosts just as well as we see normal people." He glanced at me and shrugged. "Well, everyone here does."

He frowned, eyes narrowed. "She looks pretty scared. I can't hear her, but I think she's calling for something, someone. You can't see her at all?"

"Of course I can't see her," I snapped. "I'm not a sorceress. I have no magic."

Jack grabbed my arm, shook it lightly. "What does it take to convince you? You have seen these visions for a reason, it's a gift. If you don't use the power you have, this will never end. What is it you fear so much, that you don't fear losing your parents and your friends more?"

His words fell like a blow to my heart.

"I am a healer, the daughter of healers." I whispered.

"I'm not saying you aren't. But you're something else as well. It's like saying you're a bear and a girl. One doesn't cancel out the other." He stopped for a moment, then continued, his voice lower. "Like me being a boy doesn't mean I'm not still a dog."

I stared at him, stared through him, thought of my family, how much change bothered them. And how badly I had underestimated them before. I could not hide behind the possibility of their disapproval. If I were afraid to change, I would have to acknowledge that fear, face it.

"You are right. We must——no, I must find a way to make this right."

He gripped my hand tighter. "I'm not sure what I can do, but I'm not leaving you."

The plan of not returning with the bus took time to develop and when we executed it, it happened with almost disappointing smoothness after our worries.

After an hour or two the people we had arrived with filed back into their buses and rode away. The protesters abandoned their post. As the light faded from the day, the rest of the people left in little groups. We kept out of sight. We moved into the treeline and stayed still. We Waited. Watched. Dusk came and the old pueblo was once again abandoned by everyone but us.

Free to move about without risk of discovery, we set up camp in a clearing in the trees.

"Do you want a fire?"

Jack shook his head. "I think it's warm enough for me without it. It would only give people one more thing to notice. Will you be okay?"

I nodded. "I was thinking the same thing, but wanted to make it easy on you."

He threw a handful of old pine needles at me, laughing.

While Jack rummaged through the backpack, I sat with my back to a tree, looking out over the pueblo, trapped in the loops of my mind. I tried to figure out how to reach the girl, but nothing came to me.

"Here." Jack shoved a battered sandwich and an apple at me. "Maggie restocked us last night at the house."

He turned back to the backpack, continued fishing things out with one hand while he ate.

"Flashlight, maps, bus routes." He pressed a button on a yellow-and-black cylinder and light came out, not much, but enough to read the maps.

"I'm going to assume that you'll get this figured out

tonight. My part of the job will be figuring out how to get us home once you do."

Oh. My cheeks burned. I had been so wrapped up in the problem of Isabel I hadn't thought that far ahead.

I chewed my dinner in small bites, the juices from the apple helping to wash down the dry cheese sandwich.

As I ate the last quarter of sandwich, a soft sound startled me. A black-and-white kitten with golden eyes, a pink nose and a huge plume of a tail stared at me. No, he stared at my sandwich.

I slowly took the cheese out of the bread and broke the slice into tiny pieces.

"Jack." I whispered. "Look up, but don't move."

He flicked his eyes up from the maps, scanned the area, found the cat, froze. "Cat." His nostrils flared and his eyes widened. "Cat."

"Jack, stop. This is the same cat that is in my visions. This is Isabel's cat."

CHAPTER ELEVEN

MY WORDS BROKE THE SPELL the cat's presence had placed on him. Jack glanced away from where the cat finished with the cheese and had moved on to licking the bread.

"What?"

"This is the cat that I see Isabel holding. This is her cat."

Jack looked again. "That can't be the same cat. Cats don't live that long. Isabel's cat would be hundreds of years old by now."

I shook my head. "All right. Maybe it's the son of that cat, or the grandson, or the great-great-however many time grandson. But I'm telling you, even though it's smaller, it's the same—the markings, the colors, even that ridiculous tail."

The cat glanced up at me, as if perfectly aware I had cast aspersions on his perfection. It carefully stalked around our little camp and swished its tail in front of Jack. Nothing could have been more deliberate. Jack fought to stay still.

"Bear Girl..."

"I know, he's being difficult. Please, ignore him."

Jack looked at me. "You have no idea what you're asking, do you?"

But he remained where he was and eventually the black-and-white ball of fur finished his circuit. Two white paws landed on my leg and golden eyes blinked at me.

"Come on, then." I patted my lap and the cat jumped

up, turned about, then settled down, tail wrapped around his body until it covered his nose.

I petted the furry ball. The resulting low rumble was soothing, but I still could not focus.

Jack looked up from his maps. "When Maggie can't figure something out, she'll talk to me about it. Even when I'm in my other shape and can't answer, she says it helps to get pieces straight. You could try it."

Perhaps hearing the problem aloud, instead of circling around it in my mind would help. "All right. Here are the pieces of my broken pot that I am now trying to reassemble to see the pattern."

Jack sat up, all attention. I could almost see his ears prick forwards and I smothered a smile.

"I am having visions of a girl who lived at this mission."

Jack nodded, took a bite of the apple he had saved for dessert.

"This mission was later abandoned. Recently, Maggie's father's people disturbed a grave with two skeletons. We do not know for certain that one of the skeletons was that of Isabel, but it seems likely. It also seems likely that the disturbance of the grave happened about the same time that the crying wind started in my land."

"Not that we can tell for certain," Jack interjected. "The time difference is a mess." He cocked his head. "I wonder if we could figure out exactly what the difference is? Has any one tried?"

"Jack, until recently, no one was going back and forth often enough for it to make a difference. So, no, I do not think so."

"Hmm. I wish I could make a chart or a graph, like in Maggie's schoolbooks."

His eyes focused past me and I felt a moment's frustration. "Jack? Can you make that, whatever it is, later?"

"Oh, sure." He flicked a flustered smile. "Sorry."

I returned to my pieces. "So, we think the disturbance of the grave caused the wind. Spider Old Woman thought the cry might be a heart in pain, a call for help." I stroked the cat's ears.

"From what I have seen, I think the girl is in danger from the boy, Tomás. He is not gentle with her, he tells her what he wants her to do, he frightens her." I paused, narrowed my eyes. "My first vision was of her running, afraid. I think she calls for help, for someone to hide her."

A gasp from beside me. "You think he hurt her? That he killed her?"

"I do not know. It would explain why the skeleton was in that hole. I know he took her there once. Perhaps he hid her body there."

"But," Jack frowned. "Who does the other skeleton belong to?"

"I do not know," I repeated. "I do not know anything for certain. But she ran, calling. Maybe her call was for help and she knew of no one to help but her people's legends. If she had much magic, perhaps her call echoed in the kiva and then was set free," I waved my hand at the excavation site, "by all of this."

I shook my head and the fall of hair woke the cat, who proceeded to swat at it with a soft paw. "There is something wrong here, too many pieces I do not understand. But perhaps I do not need to. If I can speak with her, she can tell me and we can solve whatever it is that has disturbed her so."

I could see my doubts mirrored on Jack's face for an instant, then he put them away.

"Then you had better get started, hadn't you?"

I wished I knew how. I sat with my eyes half-closed and tried to think about nothing in particular, to keep my mind clear. But like standing in a stream, stray thoughts, like swift, silver fish darted about. My parents, Ash, his village, Maggie's unhappiness at being left out of this,

Jack and his problem. Then the swarm of my thoughts slowed, my breathing eased. My hand stilled on the warm back of the cat and my eyes unfocused.

This time I was aware of myself as a ghost in a small room, lit through two windows shaped out of the adobe, their squares framed with wooden shutters.

In one corner of the room a curved fireplace bulged out, but no flames licked forth on this summer day. Nearby sat a massive gray chest of iron strips woven with hardened leather, the ends bearing massive twisted-metal loops as handles.

The man in the long brown robe sat at a rough hewn wooden table, hunched over papers. A large leather box sat at the upper-left corner of the table, decorated with a border of flowers and vines.

Isabel ran into the room, skirts flapping and braids flying behind her, then skidded to stop.

"Fray Alonzo, I am sorry; I did not realize you were working."

The man opened the box, took a handful of sand and gently scattered it upon the paper in front of him.

"No matter, child. I am finished now." He gently picked up the paper and let the sand run back into the box. "Now, what is so important?"

"I," she stopped. "I think we should leave this place. We should go away, go back to Santa Fe."

The man sat upright. "Why would we do that? How could we? This is our place, our home. And you, child, this is your place as well. Your father entrusted your care to me. You are too young to have been left alone at his ranch, with no one to guide you. What else could he do, since your mother left us in your infancy?"

The girl was awkward, hesitant. "Father, I think the people of the village are angry with us."

"Nonsense. Your mother was of this village and she was a true lamb of the Church. And her people also love the

Church, just as she did. All is well. When the bells ring, they come to Mass with shining faces. I will not abandon them and do not understand how you can ask me to. What has prompted this?"

The girl looked down, stared at the hard-packed floor, ran her hands over her arms. I tried to move close to her, but felt as if I walked against the stream of a river, each step a struggle.

"Tomás. He spoke to me, he said, he said... ."

The man placed one hand on her shoulder, and with the other, raised her face to his. "Child, if he has frightened you, if he has hurt you, you must tell me."

Isabel shook her head, but remained mute.

"I will speak to him, tell him he is to leave you alone from this time forth. This has gone too far."

And with that the tall man strode from the room.

Isabel stood before me, her hands in front of her face, soft sobs escaping from her.

I tried to reach her again, fought my way to her side. "Isabel! Isabel, can you hear me?"

But she did not react, not even when I reached out and gripped her upper arm. I could feel her arm beneath my hand, slim and warm, but even when I shook her, she did not notice me. She turned and left me alone in the room, standing in the sunlight.

I woke to the darkness of the trees that surrounded us. The last of the day's light had long ago left us while I traveled through the past.

"Jack, I cannot do it, I tried, but I cannot reach her, I cannot find a way to talk to her." My throat felt dry and tight, frustration threatened to turn into tears.

"Try again," Jack said. "Keep trying, you'll find a way, I'm sure of it."

I looked past the dark outlines of the trees against the sky, tried to make out patterns in the stars beyond. After a while I could feel the knots around my spine loosen.

Jack must have noticed as well. "Ready to try again?"

"No, but I have no choice, do I?"

He shook his head and grimaced.

I sat, but this time focused on what I wished to do, what needed to happen. Reality must be created out of layers; I must make a new reality. The vision, the past, the worlds here and now, the live girl, the ghost—I must mix each together with care.

Back to the beginning, back to the vision in my parents' home. She ran through fire, calling for someone, searching. I brought that image to my mind, held it, then drew an image of myself into that memory, just as I held the images of my shape when I changed forms. I shifted my memory, drew it around me, until I followed her, watched her run through the narrow hallway, push doors open, come back to the long hallway, run more. I moved myself through the memory/vision, stood in front of her.

"Isabel!"

She did not hear me.

I reached through the flame to where she stood, trapped, her eyes casting around for a way to escape.

"Isabel, take my hand!"

She jerked back from me and I wished I had thought to take a shape familiar to her, perhaps the man I had seen her talking with. Too late now.

"Isabel, please!"

She looked at me again, face pale as the moon, dark eyes wide and then, beyond all my hopes, she reached for my hand.

I grabbed her slim fingers and with all my strength, and wrenched her out. Away from the fire, away from the hall, from the memory, into a new place, all of my shaping.

I imagined a cloudy sky with a waxing moon which cast gentle light upon us. Thin grasses brushed my knees and distant trees ringed the clearing, an echo of the one in which Jack, the kitten and I sat.

She looked around, startled.

I collapsed into a heap on the ground, the pounding in my ears bringing the taste of blood to my mouth.

Hesitantly, she stepped towards me. "Are you all right?"

I gasped for air, pushed myself upright with one hand. The other hand twined itself though the soft fur of the kitten I somehow still held in my lap. "Yes, thank you. I will be fine. Are you well?"

She looked lost, but there was no fear, no wonder at this new place. As if she dreamed and had no fears about the changes in the place of her dreaming. "I think so. I, I don't remember. Was I here before?"

I watched her as she wandered away from me, then came back, her face a blank mask. "No, I do not believe you have been here before. Do you remember nothing of what happened?"

"I was running somewhere, I was scared." She wandered away again, glancing around her, her brows drawn together. "I was looking for something, but I couldn't find it anywhere. I've been looking for a long time, I think."

"Isabel," and then I stopped. If she did not remember her death and the betrayal I suspected had led up to it, was it needful for me to remind her?

For the first time she looked closely at me, focused clearly.

"I am sorry, we have not been introduced." She picked up the sides of her skirts and bent her knees, bobbing up and down once, quickly. "I am Isabel de Granillo, ward of Fray Alonzo at—oh!" She gasped and I jerked back from her.

"You have him! You found my Nicco!"

She skipped forward, her face beaming, and reached for the cat in my lap.

She scooped him up before I could protest and pressed him close to her chest, burying her face in his fur. I felt the absence of him, even as I worried. Would this kill the kitten, for a ghost to hold him?

"Thank you, I have been looking for him everywhere."
She cradled the cat in her arms.

"It was very nice to meet you, but I should go now."

I scrambled to my feet, blinking. "Isabel, wait, there's
something I must tell you."

She ran towards the edge of the clearing. "I can hear
the bells for Mass. I must go now, or I will be late!"

And she passed between the trees and out of sight.

I opened my eyes to the dim gray light of early morning.
Jack knelt beside me.

"This time was different." I croaked. "I do not think she
understood me. I will have to try again." Weariness filled
me, my head ached. I did not think I could do this again,
not right away.

The cat stirred, still in my lap and my heart leapt. His
unexpected venture into my dream world had not harmed
him. Gold eyes opened, blinked, then long front legs
stretched out and pricked my legs lightly as punishment
for waking him. He stalked off into the forest without a
backward glance, black-plumed tail erect. In the slowly
growing light I could see the midnight of his tail tipped
with a sprinkle of white hairs and wondered if they had
been there the previous day.

I looked at Jack. "I do not know if I made any difference."

"I do." Jack's quiet voice carried a weight that forced
my attention back to the matter at hand. "You made
a difference."

He looked back at the site of the old mission building.
"She's gone."

CHAPTER TWELVE

J ACK PULLED ME UPRIGHT. "LET'S get out of here and then maybe take a nap for a bit. You look a mess."

I grimaced at him. "Thank you, Jack. I feel much better now."

I stretched, pulled the kinks out of my back from the long night. "We need to get back. I need to make sure that, now that she is gone, and so the source of the wind, that the illness is lifted."

I ran my fingers through my hair, frowned at the knots and tangles that had sprung up overnight, then braided the mess out of my way the best I could.

"And we should find Maggie if we can. You know she'll be wondering about us."

He had done a good job with the maps while I had been otherwise occupied the night before. Without too much walking we mounted a bus carrying us back North. I dozed in the seat and Jack woke me when we needed to change to another bus.

As I drifted off, I thought how odd it was that already I had become so accustomed to this world to be able to sleep while in the stomach of this moving monster. Or perhaps it only showed how tired I was. I felt like leather that had worn so thin you could see light through it.

The trip home felt longer than the trip out, but by midmorning we arrived back near Maggie's house.

We headed back up the trail to the tree, our hearts light. I was anxious to see the results of our work. We reached the split cottonwood tree and paused.

"Ready?" Jack said.

I nodded and, taking his hand, stepped through.

The wind knocked both of us back and I hit the bark of the cottonwood hard enough to scrape my arm through the thin shirt.

"What happened?" Jack's wide eyes roamed the land. "It's worse than before!"

I shook my head and shouted to be heard over the raging wind. "I do not know. Let us get to the village and see if we can discover anything there."

We fought against the wind as it blew and pounded us with each step, threatening to knock us from the trail, to drive us to our knees. We took turns leading the way in the hopes that one of us would provide a breakfront for the other, give the other a rest. But our plan failed, proved useless in a wind that came at us from all directions.

We reached the shelter of the village and crawled up the ladder a thin girl lowered for us.

On the roof we thanked her. She was one of the assistants I had trained before we left. I tried to speak, but she hurried inside and waved for us to follow her.

She did not say anything until we were in the tunnels beneath the buildings, the tiny flame of dished clay lanterns casting more shadow than light.

Jack pulled at my hand and whispered, but his voice was loud in the silence. "I don't understand."

The girl stopped. "The wind has been worse the last few days. More fall sick daily; the singing never stops. Even those of us who still walk, it calls to us, loss and rage, battering everything."

Her gaunt face held deep shadows beneath her eyes.

"We have some stores of grain, but we must go plant soon, or face disaster." She turned away. "But I do not know if anything will grow in this cursed weather, or in truth, how many of us there will be for the harvest."

We passed a number of rooms filled with people who lay still. Only a few people passed from one pallet to the next, checking eyes, checking for reflexes. What had happened to all my helpers?

Our guide stopped, leaned heavily against a door. I moved towards her, concerned, but she shook my hand aside. "Your friends are within." And with no other words of explanation she returned the way we had come.

Before us lay a fever-tossed Ash. Maggie knelt on the far side of him, her hand in his, her eyes bright and wild in her pale face. She stared at us as we came in and whatever we expected her to say about our missing the check-in the previous night was lost.

"You have to make him better, you have to stop this!" She brushed his hair back from his face, put her hands on his shoulders to keep his tossing form still. "I don't understand what's going on. He can't leave me, he can't!"

And then I knew the truth.

How could I have been so blind?

It was never the girl, she did not do this.

It was the boy, Tomás. The visions were of the girl, she was the key, but the boy had been the one raised in the old traditions, the one who would have the knowledge to breach the path between the worlds.

The boy who had hated to be separated from Isabel...

And we did not know where to find him, or his ghost. Jack had not seen him at the mission.

Wait.

The boy must have been the second skeleton, down in that pit.

"Bear Girl?"

I stopped cold, blocking the door, not seeing.

"I am so sorry." I checked over Ash. "I believe he will be fine. Please, trust me. All was not as it appeared."

I laughed, perhaps a bit hysterical. "Nothing was as it appeared, to be honest."

A glimmer of a plan formed in my mind.

"I think I know what to do now, but I need your help."

She looked up from Ash and blinked away the tears from her eyes.

"Anything. Just make him well."

"I know what to do now," I repeated. "But I don't know how, not exactly."

"Another vision?" Jack asked.

"No," I pulled myself upright, wrapped my arms around my ribs. "In the beginning, this will take no magic, only courage. Maggie, you have to tell me: where can I find your father's place of work at the University, and what can I offer him that will make him willing to work with us?"

Jack and I jogged back down the path. He spent no time with his friends this trip. We hoped to be able to reach the University quickly enough to find Maggie's father still there. Maggie had said her father had been working late at the University for the last few weeks to finish his part of the study of the bones before they were returned to the Pueblo Council.

We rode the bus in silence, only the desperate grip of our intertwined hands betrayed our fear.

We ran through the campus without another glance for the sculptures or anything else until we stood in front of the tan building marked with a blue sign we had seen Maggie's father enter before.

"I think this is the right place." Jack started towards the door, but I called him back.

"Wait, we can't afford to make a mistake."

I looked wildly for someone—anyone!—to confirm what the markings on the sign said, and swore that as soon as I could I would learn Maggie's writing.

A young man with long brown hair walked by.

"Excuse me."

He kept walking and I steeled myself. This was no time to worry about politeness.

"Excuse me!" This time I stood in front of him and yelled.

He jumped. "Whoa. Sorry." And pulled tiny plugs out from his ears. "What's up, kid?"

"Is that the Anthropology building? Can we find Dr. Sanger there?"

He glanced at the building, looked at me and nodded. "Yeah, that's what the sign says. You're a little old not to be able to read."

I think he meant it as a joke, but there was no time to explain.

"And Dr. Sanger? He will be there?"

"I dunno, kid. I've never been in; I'm a comp-sci major."

And with that he replaced the plugs in his ears and slouched off.

Jack and I tore through the building and looking at the doors.

Jack shouted over his shoulder. "I know what the writing for his name looks like. I'll recognize that. It's on all the mail."

"Just find it, quickly!"

The student on the bus had given us the clue. Tomás might no longer be at the ruins of Santa Catalina, his spirit might be wandering free, but we knew where to find his body. More importantly, we knew who we must talk with.

Jack called me. "Here, it's here!" He stood in front of a door, like all the others lining the hallway, with papers stuck to the front and a little square frame around more words. Jack pointed to the frame. "See. That's the name." He laughed, still a bit nervous, then rapped on the door.

"Office hours are over!" a man's voice answered. "Come back tomorrow afternoon and we can talk about your test results."

"Doctor Sanger?" I called through the door. "We are not here to talk about," I looked at Jack, who shrugged at me, "about that. We are here to talk to you about the boy and girl you are studying."

The sound of papers being shuffled was followed by steps, then the door was flung open. "Now, listen. The appropriate papers have been filed. You can protest all you want, but we need more time to finish—"

"Sir, please. I am not protesting anything. I need to talk to you, that is all."

He narrowed his eyes. "You're not here to tell me what I'm doing is wrong?"

I shook my head. "Please let us talk to you."

Frowning, he waved us into a cramped and cluttered room, packed with books and papers. He pointed to two chairs close to the door, then walked around a table and sat facing us.

"Are you sure? You look like you're here to argue with me."

Jack spoke up. "You know that's not fair. You always say that basing an opinion solely on someone's appearance, no matter their cultural background, is a mistake, and inappropriate for a scientist."

The older man blinked. "I do, do I? You look a little young to be in my classes."

Jack stuttered. "I, uh, have a friend that sits in sometimes.

Maggie's father stared at him, then returned his attention to me. You have five minutes."

Mind racing, I struggled for the words Maggie had helped me come up with, that she thought would sway her father, even against his better judgment, but now I was on my own. "Sir, I understand that some people from the tribes may be giving you difficulties about the skeletons recovered from the kiva of Santa Catalina."

He grunted. "Difficulties. Right."

"I am not one of those people. I do not believe the people whose bones you hold care what you do with them. Your world is so outside of theirs, they have no way to understand, even," I added hastily, "if their spirits were still here.

"However, I do have a request."

His jaw tensed.

"I do not believe it will interfere with your work. It is unlikely that the ritual for the dead, the four days, has been sung. Of course, it could have happened long ago, but if a proper burial had happened, the bodies would not have been left as they were."

He shook his head. "You can sing for them when they're returned."

"Please. A short time to sing over the bodies now and then we will trouble you no more. And I do not ask without having something to trade."

He removed his glasses, polished the lenses with a cloth he removed from a corner of the table. "What do you think you can offer me?"

"First, I offer to do the sing where you can see me and hear me." Maggie had told me one of her father's biggest frustrations was the secrecy of the tribes, their need to keep their own secrets. And she had told me one other thing. A weakness of her father's.

"Also, if you would like, I will tell you stories. I do not know if they are tales you already know." I waved at his walls lined with books. "But I will tell you stories until you believe my debt to you is repaid."

He sat back in his chair, glasses forgotten in his hand. "Would you let me record you?"

I looked at Jack, who shrugged. "If I did that, would you let me sing?"

"Let's get our details straight first. How long do you want to be there?"

This time it was my turn to shrug. "As long as you

will let me, but as soon as possible. Now, this afternoon, would be best."

He frowned. "There's something going on you're not telling me, isn't there?"

I could see no way to avoid telling him the truth, or at least part of it. "I believe that a great harm is being done. I believe the sooner the singing is begun, the better. I do not ask you to believe as well, but to only believe that I will not do anything to interfere with your work."

"Your offer is tempting..." but his voice trailed off. "Still. There's no way that I can let a couple of kids down there. This is a scientific lab, not a place to have a field trip."

I could feel the moment slipping away from us. "Aren't you curious? Don't you want to know what we want, and why? And don't you want to know what stories I can tell you?"

Maggie's father started to shake his head, but Jack jumped back in.

"We won't touch anything, and it's not like we'd be alone there." His voice wavered, "Please, we'll be good."

Maggie's father looked at him and raised an eyebrow. "What an odd thing to say. What's your name, young man?"

Jack mumbled and looked at his shoes.

"What was that?"

Jack looked the human man in the face, the only father he had known and despite everything I smiled with pride at his courage.

"Jack. My name is Jack, sir."

"Huh. Of all the names... ."

Doctor Sanger looked at a corner of the desk, where a picture of Maggie sat. It showed her laughing under a tree with golden leaves and Jack, as he had always been, at her side, a black-and-white bundle of energy.

He examined us again and turned his attention back to me. "You may end up telling me a number of stories, you realize." He stood up. "I need to make a phone call to cancel a meeting I wasn't looking forward to. Then I'll get a few things and we'll go down."

We descended steps, flights and flights of them, and were stopped at doors that would not open until Maggie's father ran a small card through a hole in the wall.

I whispered to Jack, "Are you all right with this? I do not know what we will find." I had seen corpses before, assisting my parents. This, I was sure, would be something far different.

He pointed with his chin towards the back of Maggie's father, walking a few paces ahead. "I've already done the hardest part. I'll stay with you."

We finally entered a cold room with metal walls covered with squares. Maggie's father walked to one square and pulled a section of the wall out. Hidden behind the square had been a narrow ledge that rolled forward, silent and smooth.

A skeleton, darkened with age, lay on the ledge.

"Isabel," whispered Jack softly so Maggie's father wouldn't overhear.

"She's not here, is she?"

He shook his head. "No, just the traces. I can see the shadow of her face on her bones, nothing more."

Relieved that I had at least done one thing right, I turned back to where Doctor Sanger pulled open another ledge.

And stepped back. I did not need Jack's smothered gasp to tell me power radiated from the thin shelf.

"Jack, tell me what you see."

"A boy, tall, dark hair, and..." His hushed voice faltered. "Bear Girl, he looks furious."

CHAPTER THIRTEEN

MAGGIE'S FATHER HAD MOVED TO a corner of the room and was rearranging objects. "Will here work?"

I nodded. "I would not wish to disturb your work further." I pointed to a black-and-silver thing with spindly legs. "What is that?"

He stopped puttering with it and turned back to me, frowning. "You said I could record you."

Jack saved me. "You mean, like TV?"

"Sound and video."

Jack nodded to me. "It'll be okay."

"As long as it does not stop my singing, I do not care."

Maggie's father finished doing whatever needed to be done to the strange device. "Now, I know you said the four days hadn't been sung. But there's no way I can leave you down here alone and if I don't come home for four days, my wife and kid will kill me."

"I do not need to be here the whole time. Please tell Jack when you need us to stop and he will tell me." I looked at Jack. "Gently, like waking someone. Do not startle me if you can avoid it, please. I think that would be... uncomfortable."

He nodded, face severe.

I sat on the cold floor in the middle of the room, between the two ledges. I fought to clear my mind, to remember the words, the patterns that needed to be built like a path between here and the far away land the dead must travel to.

I opened my mouth and it was all wrong.

The wrong sounds, no feeling of power.

Panic filled me. Surely this would not fail simply because I was not in the land of my home. I fought to remain calm, but felt my heartbeat in my hands, my feet, my head.

I put my hands to my throat, struggled with the rising fear.

And felt the cord of the necklace given to me by Spider Old Woman. Of course. Spider Old Woman had said it would not interfere with everyday speech, but this was something different, older. The words themselves had a power that should not be altered.

"Jack?"

He came over quickly.

"I'm going to take this off. I need you to hold it for me, but don't lose it. And when you wake me, give it back to me right away, all right?" He held his hands out in a cup and before I slipped the cord from around my head I said, "Thank you. I trust you."

When I resumed, the sounds flowed from me, pure, right, resonating with home, family and love.

I chanted the words, my words becoming stones, to form a path. As I sang I focused on the sad pile of bones that I knew as Tomás.

Tomás, who had seemed so angry, so impetuous to me. But his anger had never been at Isabel, my fear that he had caused her death was unfounded. Whatever the circumstances of their passing, I had to reach him now.

And so I focused again on stitching together the worlds, formed his image in my mind, shaped his presence, one stroke at a time.

And the door crashed open.

The man we had seen at the excavation site burst in, face red, mouth drawn into a fine line.

He turned to Maggie's father, shouted words I could no

longer understand.

Before Maggie's father could react, Jack strode to him, grabbed the man's arms, shook him. Pointed to me, where I sat, still singing.

The man, shocked into silence, heard me, heard my words, for the first time. His eyes widened and the color drained from his face. Without another word he spun and left the basement room.

I resumed my craft, building the image up like forming a man out of clay. Tomás had looked like this, his hair this color and length, his mouth, hard to decide. So often smiling, but easy to flash into a frown. I decided I liked him better smiling, and so left it that way.

And I built an image of myself, took a lesson from the black-and-white cat and separated myself from myself, so that part of me remained in the cold room, singing, guarded by Jack, watched by Maggie's father. And another part of me moved forward, towards the man I had built from memories and the shape of the world he had left.

There. The walls flickered, changed from the silver metal to the dark tans of adobe. Isabel ran down the hallway, calling. I could see Tomás behind her, chasing her through the fire.

I looked around in confusion. Adobe does not burn easily, what could have happened? A section of roof fell behind the running pair and I understood. The wooden poles which made up the roof had caught fire.

I moved through the fire; it could not touch me. I wished with all my heart I could quench the flames, reshape them, make none of this happen. But this part of the vision was fixed, inviolate. I could only watch and hope I understood.

"Isabel!" Tomás yelled, but she did not hear him, only ran faster through the collapsing building.

"Nicco! Nicco, where are you?"

The cat. She had been calling for the cat, searching for her pet. Not running in fear from Tomás.

She ran towards one end of the hall, fled as that section of roof collapsed in front of her, stumbled.

Tomás, his face streaked with ashes, caught her. "Isabel, we must leave. We have to get out of here now!"

With a strength that surprised me, she shook him off. "I have to find Nicco! I have to make sure he's safe. Not like..." Her voice shrilled, broke. "Frey Alonzo. Did you see? Did you see?"

What had happened to the kindly man in the long brown robe? I remembered what the student had said on the bus. Many of the priests had been killed in the revolt. Had she seen his murder? Had the shock driven her mad? My heart broke for her and still, I could do nothing but watch.

Tomás pulled her away from where the fire grew ever closer, held her while she struggled against him.

"Nicco, think about Nicco!"

She stilled, pushed back from his arms. "Where is he? I have to get Nicco out from here!"

He shook her. "That ball of fur waits for you outside. He jumped out the window right after you ran back inside. Your grandfather has him. He's safe." The flames crackled as more straw and wood caught. "But we are not!"

Isabel clung to Tomás' hand as they twisted through the smoke. But no matter which way they ran, fire blocked them.

She screeched as her skirt caught fire and Tomás beat the flames out with his hands.

Cornered, they reached the small room I had seen before. They raced for the side door, but a burning wooden beam lay across the frame. As they spun to leave, the ceiling outside of the room collapsed, trapping them.

Isabel stood still, panting like a deer who has been run to earth and has no more will to evade the hunter. Tomás ran around the perimeter of the room, knocked the last few unburned pieces of furniture away from the flames.

He stopped in front of where she stood, unseeing.

"Isabel, I do not know what to do. One thing is left and it frightens me. But I do not think we have another choice. Will you trust me?"

She did not speak, but held her hand out to his.

He led her to the corner of the room and she stood, placid, while he scrabbled at the floor and then lifted the slab of flagstone which covered the pit.

I screamed at them, tried to stop them. But they could not hear me; this part of the story must also stay unchanged. I wanted to run, to close my eyes, to see no more. But I had to know, had to understand. And so I watched, helpless.

They had no lantern this time, but he grabbed at a long piece of wood that had fallen, lit the end at the flames licking through the room, gave the makeshift torch to Isabel and guided her down the ladder.

The beams above his head creaked and popped. He descended into the hole, pausing only to pull the flagstone back over them, as a spider lies in wait in her trap.

Within moments, the roof collapsed. I forced myself, in this body where I now played the ghost, to cross through the flames, to pass through the stone, to see them, to know the end of this horror.

By the faint light of the torch they huddled together. She stared blankly at the flame and he held her close.

"I will protect you," he murmured.

They sat, waiting. Tendrils of smoke reached through the cracks around the stone cover and spilled down, like silent assassins towards the couple below. They sat, unnoticing; she unseeing, he seeing only her.

"We will wait here and it will burn out, pass us by. I will stay with you. We will not be separated. By all the powers, all the pinang that may be. I will not leave you."

There it was. They had been separated, studied, removed from their resting place.

And then I had separated them further, by sending

Isabel away from the home she had haunted all those years.

He noticed the smoke, turned from it, stroked her hair. "Hear me, ancestors of our people. Help us. Avenge us. Do not let us be separated, from now until the world grows cold, until the flood rises and the skies fall."

I faded away. I did not want to see any more. I knew what had happened, what my presumption had made worse, how this tragedy had ended. Yet, it had not ended. His death wish would bring more sorrow if I did not stop this now.

I brought to my mind the clearing in the trees where I had spoken with Isabel. And then shaped Tomás there, standing in front of me. I did not shape him as I had seen him last, frightened, exhausted, faced smeared with ash and clothing singed, but as I had first seen him when he ran into the mission and stopped to speak with Isabel, light on his feet, happy with the world.

He stood before me now and turned slowly to look around him.

I held my breath, hoped against hope that his spirit would have more sense than poor Isabel, that her confusion lay rooted in the shock she had received prior to her death, that spirits of the dead did not always act as she did.

Tomás returned his gaze to me. In his stare was keenness of mind.

"Who are you?" His voice was sharp. "Why have you brought me here?"

He stepped towards me. Though I knew he was not the threat I had imagined him to be, I stepped back.

"I am not your enemy; I am here to help you. I do not know what you remember, but you called for help. Your call was heard, I am here."

His face creased. "I called... . I called when..." He spun around. "Where is Isabel? I promised to take care of her!"

"She is resting; she is safe."

His eyes narrowed. "Where. Is. She."

"She is safe, but you must listen to me. Do you remember what happened? The fire at the mission? Tomás, the fire was many years ago. But you called and I came. There is no need to call for help anymore."

He brushed me aside. "I'm not calling." He shook his head, continued his search for Isabel.

"You may not realize, but in the fire, you used a great amount of pinang, you——"

He shouted, "Why are you talking to me about this? Where is Isabel?" He reached towards me again.

"Isabel is dead, Tomás." I cried as I dodged his arms. "She's gone. You're dead too, and now you're killing more people."

He froze. "Say that again." He stepped backwards. "Say it!"

"She... you... you both died that day." Shock and disbelief warred on his face. "She's not scared anymore. But now other people are hurt by what you did."

His knees buckled and he sank to the ground. "It was my death curse, wasn't it? A call for vengeance, for help, to keep us together." He bowed forward, put his head into his hands. "I failed. I promised to keep her safe."

I knelt beside him. "You did your best to protect her." I placed one hand on his shoulder, soft as down. "But people have found the place you took refuge, and in..." I searched for the right words, "in their preparations for your burial, they have separated you and Isabel. Only," I hastened to add in the face of his renewed fury, "for a short time. But they had to separate your bodies in order to give you burial. They did not mean harm, only to show respect. Yet..."

He spoke for me. "Yet it was enough, enough to awaken the curse." He looked up, tears streaking his face. "Where is she?"

"She's gone, she did not wait for the singing. I found her and she, she was confused."

Hurt and comprehension warred in his face.

I tightened my hand on his shoulder. "I found her spirit. She was looking for Nicco. I don't think she remembers the end. You did well. You protected her."

His mouth twisted. "Her and that cat." He took a breath, calmed himself. "Now what? Can I follow her?"

I shook my head. "I do not know why you should not be able to. I will sing for you, so you can be free of here. But I do have a favor to ask of you."

He nodded for me to continue.

"While I sing for you, be patient with me. I have not done this before on my own. And please, try to end your curse. The breaking of your heart has shattered my homeland. All who hear your cry fall ill. What happened to Isabel, to you, was terrible. Please, let it end now."

I could see the muscle in his jaw twitch, but he nodded.

"Then I will sing the full four days and you will pass and trouble the world of the living no more."

The ritual words felt awkward on my tongue, but satisfied him.

I let the shaping of the clearing begin to fade from my mind, until he and I stood in nothing but fog.

He spoke once more.

"I never meant harm. I only loved her."

I brought myself back long enough to answer. "I know that now. I wish I had known sooner. Go when you can. I am sure she will be waiting for you."

I sat on ground I could no longer see, closed my eyes, and listened for the faint sound of chanting, of my own singing. I chanted along with myself, my voice split into harmony, then resolving into one voice, one singer, one person.

I opened my eyes. I sat on the floor of the cold room, while Jack stood by me, his face concerned.

I brought the song to a close, a place of pause. The work was far from over, but starting had been the hardest part.

My voice stilled and the silence of the room rang loud.

Jack held the pouch towards me, but did not ask me anything until I had slipped the braided cord over my head and nestled the bag under my shirt.

Then his whisper spilled like water down a hill.

"Are you all right? Is he all right? Is it over?"

My throat felt as if I had drunk sand. "No," I coughed. "We've only begun."

Maggie's father did something with his device, then walked towards us.

"Thank you. I doubt anyone else has footage of that ceremony."

He reached for my hand and pulled me to my feet.

"Please understand that each family may sing for the dead differently."

Maggie's father slid Isabel's ledge back into the wall and moved towards Tomás. I put my hand on his arm to stop him.

"Dr. Sanger, I need to ask you one more favor."

He looked as if I'd handed him a snake.

"Please do not separate them further, see that they are kept together as much as you can. It is all they ever wanted. Do not deny them."

He looked at me for long moments before answering. His eyebrows raised, and I could guess some of the stories he would ask of me might be different from the ones I had expected to barter.

A curt nod and we were on our way back out of the basement laboratory. I walked slowly, thankful that Dr. Sanger was caught up in his own concerns.

We came to one of the heavy metal doors and I stood in front of it, too exhausted to fight with its weight. Jack opened it, then stood aside to let me pass through.

"Thank you, Jack." I whispered.

Maggie's father heard me, turned to us.

"You know, it's a funny thing. I know that's a common

name, but it was the final straw that made me decide to take a chance with you." He grinned, startlingly like Maggie. "No offense, but my daughter's dog has that name. He ran away a few days ago and she's heartbroken. They've never been separated before and her mom and I don't know what to do. I'm not a superstitious man, but I guess I took your name as an omen. I always trusted our Jack, figured I'd trust you."

He reached his office and stopped to unlock the door. Behind him Jack and I cast frantic glances at each other. How could he have guessed?

"Sorry, I'm rambling." He stepped into his office and we stayed in the hall. He called out. "How is sometime next week for some of those stories?"

I shrugged. "It is difficult for me to tell when I will be here, but I will try."

When Maggie and I had struck upon the idea that I could trade information with her father, we had not figured out how I would know when to come back.

Jack spoke up. "I can remind you and bring you back."

Maggie's father nodded. "Well, that should work." He walked back to his desk and waved his hands at the piles of paperwork. "I should call Mr. Sanchez from the Pueblo Center, clarify what we were doing, smooth that out. But you know what?" He grabbed a coat from a hook on the wall and came back out to the hall where we waited. "I'm going home to my wife and daughter."

On the bus the exhaustion fell on me like a load of wood. Tears fell and I stared out the window, crying.

Jack wrapped his arm around my shoulders and held me. "What do we do now? How are you going to finish the singing? Isn't it supposed to be four days?"

"It is; it will be. But for once the time difference will help us."

We walked up the trail in silence, crossed through the tree and felt the wind against us. It seemed quieter, but I could no longer tell.

I sat, put my back against the passage tree, handed Jack my necklace and started to chant.

The days rolled by, I slept little, but fell into a deep trance. Not like when I had shaped the clearing to talk with Tomás, but restful, easy, like running for miles and miles.

Jack stayed with me the first day only leaving once when he ran to the village for a small pot of water. I sipped it to keep my throat clear.

After the first day Jack brought some of the healthy ones from the village to where I sat and their voices joined with mine. They did not know Tomás, but it could not hurt that others, even strangers, sought to give honor to the dead.

And we sang and sang and finally it was over.

CHAPTER FOURTEEN

THE ABSENCE OF THE WIND echoed in my ears as I woke. Jack sat propped against an adobe wall, sound asleep in a beam of light from a high window that flooded a corner of the room.

I got out of the blankets and passed him silently. I was sure he had slept as little as I had during the sing. I passed from the adobe-walled room into the adjoining one. Ash and Maggie talked in hushed voices, but stopped when they saw me.

Maggie pushed herself to her feet and came to where I leaned just inside the door. "Jack told me a little of what you did. Thank you."

I embraced her, but felt hollow, strange inside. "I wish I had seen the truth sooner. I do not know if the wind killed any, but because I was slow in my understanding, more fell ill than would have."

Ash spoke. "Like me?" He shook his head. "Bear Girl, you did what you could. No one could have known what happened, so long ago, so far from here."

I looked at him, but could only see Tomás and Isabel as they had been at the end, huddled in the dying light, the smoke wrapping around them.

"Hey."

I blinked and again saw Maggie in front of me.

"You should go rest more."

"No, I need to check on my patients and see how people fare."

She smiled. "You taught your assistants well. We've already checked on all the villagers who fell ill to the wind. Even the worst are now sleeping peacefully and many are already awake."

"My mother is up, making soup, already asking when we are going to get on with the spring planting," Ash added with a grin.

"Then I should go back to my parents' home. They will be worried."

"A message has already been sent to them and they have sent messages of their own. They know you are here and are well. Really," Maggie's brows drew together as she searched my face, "there is nothing you must do right now."

"Except rest more." Jack spoke from behind me and put his arm around my waist to guide me back to the pallet.

I protested, there were things that must be done, I had to...

He refused to listen. "Your only responsibility right now is to rest. Later we'll talk." His eyes lowered. "We'll all talk. And I'll need you then."

I woke again and watched the last of the light scattered across the floor. I did not see Jack this time, but heard low whispers from next door.

When I woke the third time, sunlight again streamed through the window. A large covered basket sat next to where Jack lay watching me. I reached towards it but he grabbed my wrist.

"But, what is inside?"

He opened the lid, just a crack, for me to peer in.

Later, all four of us sat outside underneath the spreading arms of the ancient shade tree in the middle of Ash's village, just now putting forth pale green buds.

Throughout the day the village had come back to life as the last sleepers woke. Ash's mother had held me as she told me of the death of two of the oldest ones. Even knowing there was nothing I could have done, their loss cut me.

We had spent the rest of the long morning telling our stories. At the end, Maggie spoke. "I still don't understand how his call for help could have gotten so twisted. How could something there affect people here?"

Jack answered first. "I've been thinking about that a lot. I think Tomás' call for help should have come here back then, to where Spider Old Woman and Coyote are. But the collapse of the church in the fire sealed it in somehow. And the magic circled around and around, like a dust devil."

"Until they opened the graves," Ash whispered. "And then it swept over our land as the crying wind."

Maggie pulled her backpack to her. "Come on, Jack. It's time for us to get home. Let's see what we can tell Mom and Dad this time."

She stood and brushed off her pants, but he only put a hand out to stop her. "Wait. We need to talk."

She looked confused. "We can talk on the way home, right?"

"No, Maggie. We need to talk here, now, with our friends."

She sat back down, a pout on her lips. "All right. I know we need to figure out how we're going to work things. I know I can't keep abandoning you when I go to school. And I'm sorry that I didn't think about it before."

Jack took one deep breath, another. "Maggie. I can't go home with you."

"What?"

"Please, let me say it all at once. This is hard, so hard,

but I can't. So, let me say it one time and be done."

She stared at him in disbelief, shocked into silence.

"Maggie, how old am I?"

"Um, you're three, maybe four?"

"Do I look that young to you?"

"No, of course not. Dogs age differently..." She faded off.

He looked away from her pain. "I can't stay with you. I don't know if things will be different here, but I know that in the year since Shriveled Corn Man changed me, I've gone from being younger than you to older. How old will I be next year? How long until I'm older than Mom and Dad? I've got to stay here, where someone might have an answer."

Tears welled in Maggie's eyes and I placed my hand on Jack's arm. "Enough." I whispered. "She understands."

"I can still come visit if you want. You're still my sister, my best friend." A faint smile crossed his face. "I didn't mind waiting for you. I would have done it forever. But here I can do things. I don't know for how long, but I can have a life where everyone knows what I am, what I can do."

She stayed silent.

"Maggie? Can I still come visit?"

She flung herself forward, breathing in loud racking sobs.

"Maggie?" Jack's face filled with panic. Ash stroked her back, waited for the tears to subside. "Maggie, please stop? I have something for you."

She sat up, sniffing. "First," she said. "I want you to know I'm not mad at you. Just angry that it has to be this way, that you're right. But not mad with you. And yes, come visit. You better visit lots, or I'll never forgive you."

He touched her hand lightly. "Good. It'll be nice to see Mom and Dad too. It was neat to see where he works. I thought for a minute he guessed about me, at the very end. Anyhow." Jack pulled the large basket out from behind the tree. "You do not have to accept this. You may not be ready. If so, I will keep it, so please don't feel there's an obligation."

Maggie shook her head. "Whatever it is, I'm sure I'll love it. You're as bad as Dad when he's agonizing over birthday presents."

She reached for the basket, then pulled her hands back sharply.

"Jack, did it just move? What is it?"

He cracked open the woven lid, peeked inside, and then handed her a black-and-white kitten, with a long plume of a tail.

"I went back for him. After everything, it seemed right that Nicco, or Nicco's grandson, stay with one of us. I could not leave him alone in those trees. I think perhaps that line of cats stayed there because they sensed the spirit of Isabel. But with her gone from that place..." he shrugged.

Maggie took the fuzzy bundle from him and bent over it, crying anew.

"It is not much, but something small to fill the hole in your heart."

The kitten mewed and washed the tears from Maggie's cheeks until they stopped, then curled into a ball of fluff. Ash reached over to stroke its sleeping body. "He is very soft." An evil twinkle lit his eyes. "I would think he would make a great pair of slippers. Or even mittens. If there was enough to go around."

Maggie swatted him gently, so as not to disturb the kitten. "Don't even think about it!" Her weak smile relieved us all. At the sight of it Jack's shoulders slumped with relief. Along with her parents, Maggie was the most important person in his life. To change that relationship took more courage than I had, for I had not yet discovered a way to change the relationship with my own parents.

Tired again, I lay back on the ground and watched the wisps of clouds across the deep-blue sky as they skidded along, caught by a wind so far above us that all we felt was the faintest breeze.

"So, what now?" asked Ash.

"Now?" I echoed. "Now, I need to go home. After that?" I shrugged, although from where I lay it was unlikely anyone could see me. "Who knows."

"Bear Girl?" Jack's voice was soft.

"Hmm?" I could feel myself lulled back to sleep by the warmth of the sun.

"Would you mind if I traveled back with you? I haven't seen much of the land and would like to get to know more people, more of how things work here, before I settle down somewhere."

Ash spoke up, "You know you always have a home in the village."

Then he grunted, as if someone had kicked him. I drifted further into sleep, but made myself mumble an answer. "Of course. Come visit my parents; they will have ideas on what you can do. They always have ideas for what is best for me."

I fell into the blackness, but heard Jack chuckle. "Not so different from home, then."

That night Maggie left, after making one further promise.

"She is not a bad person." I begged. "She is only a little difficult some days. Or most days. But Spider Old Woman wants to know how you are doing. If she did not, she never would have asked me."

"She could just show up in my dreams again." Maggie grumbled.

"She could, but she has not. I would take that to indicate she would like to see you in the flesh. You know there is a difference."

She nodded and I decided not to push my advantage too far. I hugged her and reached into the basket for a final pat of the kitten. Maggie had decided to name him Nicco the Twenty-Eighth, for we had no idea how many generations might separate him from his namesake.

The golden eyes blinked lazily, then he retreated back to the shadows of his basket.

"Mom and Dad aren't allergic, are they?" Jack worried.

"No, why?"

"Remember when we were little and our neighbor's cat had kittens? You wanted one and Mom wouldn't let you."

Maggie laughed. "Silly, that was because they thought you would eat it."

He flushed. "I wouldn't have... well, maybe."

Ash took the basket from her and started down the path. "Come on. If you have to leave, let's go. Otherwise you'll stay here talking half the night."

"I will not!"

We could hear them bickering long after they walked out of sight.

"It's funny."

"Hmmm?" I turned to look at Jack.

"Sometimes I think they like each other. And then sometimes they act like that."

I laughed. "I think the times they act like that prove they do like each other."

He shook his head. "Weird."

We did not leave the village until mid-morning the next day. Ash had returned and the three of us talked long into the night, far longer than we should have. But it was nice to have time to talk, to laugh, without the pressure of solving any mystery.

I gathered my bear coat from Ash's mother's arms. She had kept it safe for me through everything. "Thank you." I buried my face in the fur, again grateful beyond measure to be back near my own skin.

Ash's mother packed a basket for us to take back. "Now, none of your arguments, young woman. Your parents have sent us much help over the years, and I am sure that after the ordeal of the last few weeks they are exhausted. This should help restock their larder, give them a bit more of a break. Besides," she continued, "some of those bundles are for Spider Old Woman. I've put her mark on them so you can be sure."

She must have seen something in my face. "You are going to see her straightaway, aren't you?"

I had not thought of it, no. I had only thought to go home, to see my parents, have my life return safe and normal. "In a few days, perhaps..." my voice trailed off, as I could see from her expression that I had given the wrong response.

"Or, I could go right away. But the house of my parents is on the way."

"Well, of course, girl. Go see your parents, but if you can, continue on to see Grandmother. Though she already must know the results of your task," and she waved her hands through the still air, an odd reminder of the absence of the wind. "You know perfectly well she wants all the details and does not like to be kept waiting."

Like Maggie, I was surprised that Spider Old Woman had not visited my dreams to gather the information herself. Much faster that way, but I was grateful for her absence. I had enough of strange dreams and visions for a while.

CHAPTER FIFTEEN

I WAS TEMPTED TO STRETCH OUT the trip back to my parents' home. From a distance the land appears to be covered in a veil of light green mist, but upon closer inspection the scrub is only putting forth the barest leaf buds, the sparse grasses just coming into their growth. Birds filled the sky and their loud voices at dawn and dusk made conversation impossible. Walking in silence with Jack soothed me and to watch him watch the land made me smile.

He had insisted on carrying the basket for me, even though in bear shape I could carry its weight without thinking twice. But he asked that we stay in our human shapes while we traveled. It would be easier to point out features of the landscape if I had hands and fingers.

"You know, once we change, I'll be bigger than you."

He shrugged. "Yup." Then he grinned. "But I don't have to wear a fur coat around everywhere. Aren't you roasting in that thing?"

I shook my head. "How can I be hot in my own skin? That is just weird."

"'Weird,' she says."

And I hit him on the arm, much as I had just seen Maggie do to Ash.

My parents waited for us outside the cliff door.

I ran to their arms and Jack held back, giving us a moment.

After a little crying and my father's embrace that was almost enough to crack my ribs in this form, I stood back.

"How did you know we were coming?" I looked from one to the other, their smiling faces, relaxed and happy, so different from how I had last seen them.

My mother laughed, that fluttering trill I had feared to never hear again. "Spider Old Woman came to me. She told us you would be here today, at the hour when the sun touched the top of that tree."

She pointed and I turned to see the edge of the disk of the sun just resting on the top of a pine tree that stood by itself, a short distance apart from all the others. "And here you are!"

My father walked to where Jack clutched the basket to his chest. "Thank you."

Jack blinked, looked startled. "Sir?"

"I thank you for your care of our daughter. We have been told that you did much for her safety. Gave up much for her."

Jack looked at the ground, stammered a bit. I crossed over to them quickly, hoping to rescue him.

"Father, Ash's mother has sent you many things. Shall we bring them inside? Some are for Spider Old Woman." I paused, drew breath, spoke quickly. "She asked that I bring them to her as soon as possible, I was thinking we could leave——"

My mother interrupted. "Leave? I do not think so, cub."

"But," I stood, shocked. After all I had been through, seen, done, was I still to be treated like a cub?

My mother must have seen what I was thinking, for the smile she had fought to control burst forth. "Silly girl. You do not think that your father and I would keep you to ourselves now, do you?"

My mind reeled. I was not sure what to think.

"You do not need to travel to see Spider Old Woman. She is here."

She gestured towards the opening of the cave.

"Here?" I echoed. "In our home? I thought you meant she told you we were coming in a dream."

My mother laughed at my surprise. "Well, daughter, what are you waiting for?" Father scooped the basket from Jack's grasp and held it lightly under one arm. His other hand rested gently on Jack's shoulder, as if to try to reassure him. I found myself disturbed by Spider Old Woman at the best of times.

I was wrong about Jack, though. Quick as thought he slipped out from under my father's hand and went to her arms.

"Grandmother! It is so good to see you."

He had spent time with her while waiting for Maggie once. He must have had a good memory of that time for him to be so comfortable with her now.

I expected her usual sharp rebuffs to be directed at Jack's exuberance, but she smiled and held him close to her.

"It is good to see you as well, boy. I am pleased you have decided to stay with us. I am proud of you."

He beamed down at her and I realized how small she stood, leaning against his height.

He stepped back, expecting me to hug her as well. I had never dreamed of taking such a liberty, but would not back down in front of him. She gave a brief nod and I gently embraced her thin shoulders.

I handed her the charm she had given me so long ago. "Thank you, Grandmother. Your words started me on the right path to solve the problem. You were right. The cry was of loss and heartbreak, but never meant evil."

"All right. Enough time for stories once we're all inside," my father boomed.

And we did not talk of anything more serious than the fish Spider Old Woman had seen in the river, or the crows that flocked north of our home, or what the year's harvest might bring, until after dinner and after the packages and bundles Ash's mother sent had been sorted and the ones for our family put neatly away.

I went to fetch more wood for the fire and Jack came with me. We walked through the gathering evening, the purple streaks across the sky highlighted by navy blue, the blue fading deeper to black, sprinkled with countless stars, like all the fish ever imagined in a black, endless river.

"Your parents are nice," Jack commented. "They're a lot like Maggie's. Well, sort of. They're a lot different too, but that might be because of how different things are here. I wonder..."

I could hear his thoughts start, just like when he wondered if anyone had ever figured out a set of correspondence tables for how the time flow worked.

"Wonder later, Jack. Right now, we need to finish gathering the wood and get inside." I brushed my hand over his hair. "But you are right, they are nice. And it pleases me to know you like them."

Inside, my parents and Spider Old Woman sat as I related the story of all we had done, of the decisions we had made, the mistakes I had made. Jack picked up the story where I could not focus my thoughts on how it had happened. It all made so little sense when it was happening to us and only now did it string together like beads on a cord.

"And so, in the end, all he wanted was help: help to protect her, to stay with Isabel."

My mother's eyes had filled with tears and my father placed his arm around her shoulders and pulled her close. "Those poor children. How terrible. How terrible for them all."

"One thing still troubles me," I turned to Spider Old Woman. "If we are not the past of Maggie's world, if we are a time set apart, where do we come from and where do people go that leave our world?" I thought of all the other people in Maggie's world, all the people that I was sure did not come from here. "Are there other worlds that connect to Maggie's? Or to our world? And can something from those other worlds affect us here, too?"

Spider Old Woman laughed. "For a girl who refuses to be anything other than a healer, you ask a number of questions that normally are only worried about by users of magic."

I flushed. "I am sorry. If this is forbidden knowledge, secret or sacred, I did not mean to trespass."

She slapped the ground. "Nonsense. Nothing should be secret to those who seek. The answers usually cannot be given in just an evening by the fire. Most of those answers take years, lifetimes to discover. And the answers are different for each person."

"But how..." My yawn interrupted my next question and my father took the opportunity to close the evening.

"I think that is enough for one night. If you decide you would like to learn more, you have other nights for that. But now, you must sleep. Grandmother, we have prepared a place for you to rest if you would like."

She shook her head. "I will stay by the fire if that is not a bother to you."

Father laughed. "Our daughter is safely home. Nothing is a bother."

Mother prepared a sleeping pallet a little ways from mine for Jack. Long after we had gone to bed, he tossed and turned.

"Just change." I whispered.

"What?"

"Just change back if you want, nobody here minds."

Taking my own advice I held the warm golden form in my head while I closed my coat, shifted to bear shape and curled into a large furry mass.

When I looked up, a sleek black-and-white dog stood before me, head cocked to one side.

"What?"

He cocked his head to the other side.

"Oh. We need to find Coyote soon, get him to teach you how to speak in both shapes. But now, what is it?"

He stepped to the side of my flank, turned in a delicate circle, lay down then looked again at me.

"I am sure my fur is a thicker mattress for you. This is fine."

Jack lowered his head between his paws and I did the same.

"Good night, Jack."

When I woke in the morning I noticed my mother standing across the room watching us sleep, rolling her head from side to side. A habit she picked up in bear form, it looked natural enough in her larger shape, but father and I teased her about doing it as a human. It was usually a sign she was deep in thought.

It took time to slide out from under Jack without waking him, but eventually I managed and went to my mother's side.

I shifted back to human form so as not to tower over her. "What?" I whispered.

She shook her head and led me outside. We waved at Spider Old Woman as we passed, but she stared at the fire and did not see us.

We sat on the greening hill outside the house and listened to the chorus of birds.

"Daughter, you know I love you, yes?"

"Of course."

"Then know that no matter your decisions and no matter where they take you, your father and I will always love you."

I shook my head, confused. "Mother, I do not understand. I am not going anywhere. Why do you talk of such a thing now that I am just come home?"

Then I thought of how I had been resting with Jack's form curled against mine. "Mother, he cannot go back to the other world. I may go visit it, now that I know how, but I would not live there, not for a million lifetimes.

"But..." I had a flash of thought, "You should go with me to visit, to see it all!"

"What!" She laughed. "Me, go to that strange place?"

"Yes, you might like it there."

"Foolish cub. What could be there that I might like?"

"The people are kind. Different from us, but perhaps not as much as we would think. Besides," I glanced at her out of the corner of my eye. "You might want to meet Maggie's parents some day."

"Oh," she said. "I see." We sat for a few moments of silence while we watched the sky lighten streak by streak.

"They would also be considered Jack's parents, would they not?" she asked.

"He thinks of them so. I do not know how they would react to the sudden news they have a son, especially a grown one. I am not so sure I want to be the one to tell them."

"But it might be interesting to meet them anyway."

"I was just thinking aloud, Mother. It would be an adventure."

She laughed again. "I think we have all had quite enough of adventures to last us for a while." She rose to her feet. "Let us go back and see if the others are stirring yet."

Everyone was indeed up and moving as we came back into the house. Spider Old Woman and Jack huddled over the fire, deep in conversation. I hesitated to interrupt, but needed to prepare breakfast.

"Are you sure?" I could hear the strain in Jack's voice.

"Boy, I have not offered something that I did not mean in more years than you should think of. I do not make offers lightly. But if you are serious about these things, this is the best way."

Though I tried not to listen, I felt a flutter of fear. Was she going to send him back, somehow change him? I could not understand why my heart beat so fast. I had lived my entire life without him. It should not matter in the least if he lived somewhere else, returned home to Maggie and the people who loved him. Yes, that would be best.

"Bear Girl, did you hear?" He grinned.

"Yes, Jack, I did."

He looked at me, confused. "Why are you upset about it?"

"I am not upset. Why do you think so?"

He looked at me and shook his head. "Your face looks upset, that's all. Anyhow, I thought you'd be happier this way." His shoulders slumped. "I guess you're not."

Clearly he had thought it was for the best and I should work harder to be less selfish. And yet, I would miss our travels through the land, talking about flowers and plants and his wild speculations as to how the universe itself worked.

"Jack," I placed a hand on his shoulder. "Whatever you think is the right thing to do, I will believe in you."

He looked further confused.

Spider Old Woman laughed. "I think we should start from the beginning. Something has gotten lost." She turned to me. "Jack is going to come live with me. Jack has these," she flung her arms out, "wild plans to discover how time works, what the source of magic is, and such and such. It is best for all of us if I can keep an eye on him. Safer, too."

I blinked, turned from one to the other of them. "He's going to go live with you?" I struggled to wrap my mind around the concept.

"Yes, what did you think we were talking about?" Jack asked.

"Oh, nothing!" I felt foolish, but too happy to care.

"I thought you might like it, since I'd be closer than if I stayed at the village." And he flushed.

I hugged him, then reached over to include Spider Old Woman. "Thank you, Grandmother," I whispered.

"You are welcome, child." She pushed away from me, her face stern. "Now, if you recall, you promised me a service."

I stiffened. She was right. I had asked for her help, with nothing to trade but a promise.

"Yes, Grandmother."

"I want two things."

Two? I could not argue. I braced, waiting to hear.

"First, I want you to consider that you have all the earmarks of becoming a practitioner of magic in your own right. You ask the right questions. You think. You are not afraid to act. And you have the talent."

I shook my head and she reached out and stopped me with one thin hand. "Just think about this. That is what I want."

"Second," she paused, and for a frightening moment resembled Coyote. "Promise to visit us often, myself and my new apprentice."

I smiled and relaxed.

"Oh yes, I can promise that."

THE END

If you enjoyed Bear Girl's story, please take a moment to review it where you purchased it, and come by my site and let me know what you think! http://www.plottingsomething.com

Please leave reviews at:
Smashwords
Amazon
or
Goodreads

Like me on Facebook to keep up with new book news and releases.

Facebook.com/coriejweaver

ABOUT THE AUTHOR:

I didn't grow up planning to be a writer. I was never one of those kids scribbling stories in a notebook, or submitting to the school paper. But I've always been a voracious reader. A few years ago, I realized I had some of my own stories to tell. I've been lucky enough to have participated in some fabulous crit groups, and to have attended the Taos Toolbox Workshop.

I love reading. I love stories of adventure, stories that grab me and won't let me go. Stories that will stay with me for years. Old and new, paper books, digital and comics – anything with a good story is fair game. And I love writing, telling stories, creating worlds and people and histories... and then doing terrible things to them!

My background is in medieval history (Spanish manuscripts of the apocalypse, if you were wondering), but as I'm fond of being able to pay the bills, I work at our local university, as well some freelance work as a web designer. I live in Las Vegas, New Mexico (the smaller, older, and much quieter one) with my husband and our two cats and two dogs. We travel as much as possible, and are active with our local animal rescue group.

Continue reading for a sneak preview of Mirror of Stone, available January 2014.

CHAPTER ONE

B Y THE MIDDLE OF THE dinner shift, Eleanor Weber
wanted to scream or die. She didn't care which.

"Girl!" shouted yet another drunken farmer
from the tavern's common room.

Eleanor raised her head from the kitchen table and
stared out the window. Ladril hung low in the cloud-filled
sky that night. The swirling pastels of the planet above
provided a dramatic backdrop for the buildings across
the street.

"Girl!" The woman's voice sounded louder, rough with
drink and impatient.

Eleanor stood up, straightened her apron and made
her way out to the front of the tavern with a loaded tray.

Wiring lay exposed in long runs down the grey ceiling,
paired with pipes that despite Eleanor's constant repairs
crackled and hissed like old women gossiping, even when
the hall stood empty. But ever since the trading ships
and their Navy escort arrived at the spaceport outside of
Prime, her father's bar had overflowed with customers.
A table of Guardsmen argued about recruitment terms,
merchants complained about grain that had spoiled in the
long delay between ships, farmers speculated on ways to
transform more of Travbon's barren rock to good soil and
everyone argued about candidates in the next election.

Eleanor could make out the faces of a handful of
regulars, but tonight most were strangers in from outlying
farms, or prospectors who had rushed into town as soon as

the news of the ships' arrival went out. Everyone seemed to be shouting, as all forms of accented Standard jumbled against Eleanor's ears.

"Here you are, ma'am," Eleanor placed the full wine glass down by the strapping woman.

The farmer didn't bother to look away from her drinking partners as she held her credit chip up for scanning.

At a far table, Mrs. Jameson shook her head at the rowdy crowd. Surrounded by miners and farmers, Mrs. Jameson gave the impression she had stepped out of some fashion vid to model the latest styles from Claro. Eleanor couldn't think of anyone else in town who would bother to stitch designer outfits out of scraps of fabric, but somehow Mrs. Jameson's efforts succeeded. The severe grey and black jumpsuit made the widow look taller, even sitting down.

"Sorry it took me so long to get here, it's a madhouse tonight." Eleanor waved her hand at the crowded room behind her.

"All going well? How's Greg? I only planned to come in for a moment, but can stay and help if you need it."

"No, it's fine. Everyone's wound up, that's all. And I'm sure my father will be down shortly. He's resting for a bit right now." Eleanor wiped down the table and looked away from the older woman's sharp gaze. *She knows. Everyone must know.*

Eleanor wished her aunt would come out from behind the scuffed bar and help serve tables, even if it meant listening to her complaints later. Susan preferred to reign from behind the bar, only emerging to break up a fight if it came down to that. With luck, this wouldn't end up being that sort of night.

Burly men in plain grey coveralls argued over a section of the map pinned to the wall. Prospectors in from the Newell Mountains to the east, by the pale lines embedded into their faces. Respirator marks. Eleanor had often seen the black molded devices when she cleaned guest rooms. Once she had placed one gingerly over her mouth and nose. It felt uncomfortable, claustrophobic and she had torn it off. Still, the awkward device formed an essential part of the miner's kit.

"Miss? Might there be a room still available?"

Eleanor jumped at the light touch on her arm. At a guess, she'd have placed the old man as another prospector. His travel-stained clothes and the rancid smell indicated it had been a while since his last bath. Not that anyone else in the place smelled much better. His matted grey hair stuck up from his head in tufts around his face.

"I'd have to check, but I think one of the smaller berths is open. Would that be all right?"

"That's fine. I'm not sure if it much matters anymore." The man slurred his words. Perhaps he had brought his own flask.

She shrugged. One fewer table to wait on. She stepped away but he waved her back.

"The Namok flooded. Took me weeks longer to get back than I'd planned. I went to Administration to tell them but they laughed me out of the office." The old man slumped over the table. His gummy eyes gazed past her, focused on something she couldn't see.

"Well, I'm sorry for that. Maybe someone in Administration will listen to you tomorrow." She stepped away. "I'll go set up that berth for you."

As she passed the bar she said to Susan, "I'm setting up a room for that old man. What's open?"

Susan snorted. "Him? Did you get his money first? He doesn't look like he can pay for his wine, much less a berth."

"Watch the front, would you? I'll take a plate to Poppa while I'm up."

Susan shrugged. "On your head, then."

The swinging of the kitchen door cut off the noise of

the front room. A few slices of smoked sausage, a piece of hard cheese, a hunk of dense bread fresh from that morning's baking. A glass of fortified water. A set of fresh sheets for the prospector's guest berth. All ready.

Upstairs, Eleanor put the tray of food on the bedside table while she made up the small room. *What an odd man. I wonder if anyone knows he's gone crazy. Maybe nobody cares enough to keep him home, out of trouble.*

She took the tray down to the end of the hall past the sputtering light that she could never get to burn evenly and around the corner to where the family's rooms clustered. She took a deep breath.

"Poppa? It's me. I brought you something to eat."

An empty bed, sheets torn off, faced her. A straight-backed chair lay overturned next to the table littered with empty bottles. The dank sweet smell of rot mixed with the sharp tang of alcohol hung in the air although Eleanor had cleaned the room yesterday. Watery light from the street outside provided the sole illumination.

"Poppa?"

A sob drew her attention to the corner behind the bed.

"There's my girl. My pretty, pretty girl."

"Come on, Poppa."

Eleanor's stomach knotted. Why did he have to be like this? Why couldn't he help, instead of leaving everything to her? He acted as if he alone had been abandoned.

"Come here, honey. Put that tray down. Maybe I'll get to it later."

She cleared space among the bottles on the cluttered table for the tray.

"At least drink the water, please?"

"That sludge? Tastes wrong."

Eleanor sighed. "I've told you. That's because it has vitamins and stuff in it. It'll help you get better."

Pretending to herself that her father stayed in his room due to sickness worked most of the time, but she couldn't lie to herself here among the bottles and the vomit.

"Come here," he repeated. "Wanna tell you a story."

"I don't have time right now. You should come on down, spend some time with everyone. Your friends miss you. They've asked about you all night."

But she cleared a space on the floor and sat next to him.

"I never met a prettier woman than your mother, not in the whole colony." His voice had faded from the baritone she loved to a ragged growl. "Martha. Such a plain name for a beautiful girl. At your age, she had dark hair and sun-gold skin, just like you. Half the boys fell over themselves to get her attention. But she picked me. Me! Never understood it."

Eleanor continued to smile and nod, but didn't listen. She had heard this story too many times. Four years earlier the Kherdan flu had ravaged the colony. Even when the supply ships had flown regularly, there had been shortages, especially of medicines. The fever left her mother frail and easily tired. Weeks would pass without her mother leaving the bedroom, weeks Eleanor remembered of creeping upstairs, peeking through the door to watch her mother sleep, waiting for each breath to come, strands of long hair cascading across the coverlet like embroidery.

She glanced at him. Her father had passed out again while lost in his memories. Over a year since her mother had finally faded away. During her own devastation, Eleanor had hated her father for surviving the final separation so well. It had been an illusion, a charade of functionality. He had been hanging on with his fingernails, waited for her to finish school, even encouraging her to graduate early, before descending into his own collapse.

She jerked the sheets back onto the mattress, then pulled and pushed until she managed to get her father in and covered by the blankets.

Not sure why I bother. He won't stay.

The next morning Eleanor served breakfast to guests as they stumbled down to the common room, bleary from the previous evening's excesses. From their looks, she guessed few had slept well; a storm had advanced up the coastline and the wind rattled the building through the night. Throughout the morning, wind pushed against the building with such force everyone sat huddled, as if they could feel the cold gusts.

She halted inside the door of the kitchen and smiled, not the weak thing she wore for the customers, but really smiled for the first time all morning.

A stocky boy with a mess of sandy brown hair pulled packages of food out of a carry-box and neatly arranged them across the counter.

"Mom said you were due for a reorder. I figured I'd bring up the regular items, save you a bit of a trip." He glanced up and the corners of his green eyes crinkled into the familiar smile.

Doug Reilly reached into the top of a large cupboard to put away zippacks of grain.

"Not there, I'll never reach them."

"Sure thing, shorty."

"How are your folks?"

"They're fine. The store's been swamped. You know all the things we've been out of? Mom's been placing calls to everyone who backordered. I hope we have enough stock to keep us through until the next ship comes." He shrugged and pushed his hair out of his eyes. "It'd be easier if we could manufacture more things here. We keep asking for machine parts, but somehow they keep getting left off the manifest. Dad thinks it's all some huge conspiracy."

Eleanor flicked her eyes to the door to the main room. "Shhh. You never know."

Doug shrugged and stowed the last of the supplies. "I

guess not, but I don't think always worrying about the monitors is going to help. How's it going for you?"

Eleanor flung herself into a chair at the kitchen table and threw her hands up. "Susan's getting bossier and Dad is getting worse. I don't know what I'm going to do, or how long I can live like this. The next person that yells 'girl' or calls me 'dear' is going to get a drink thrown in his face. And I wish Susan would go away. She means well, but we don't need her. Dad and I can do it on our own. I want Dad get back to normal; for things to be like they were before."

She stopped to catch her breath. "I sound like I'm six and want an extra candy, don't I?"

Doug walked behind her chair and put his broad hands on her shoulders. She could feel the muscles begin to relax. "El, why don't you..." He hesitated. His hands paused in their pattern.

"Why don't I what? Push Susan down the stairs? Trust me, I've thought about it. Lots."

He chuckled and kept rubbing, found little knots of tension, smoothed them out, one layer at a time.

"I'm worried about you. You know that. You can't stay here forever. It's not healthy for you." He tightened his grip over a stiff muscle and she yelped. "See?"

She sighed. "Even if you're right, what am I going to do about my father? I can't leave him."

Doug sat at the table and put his hand over hers. "I don't know what he needs. He has to want to get better, and I'm not sure he does. Honestly, are you?"

Eleanor pulled her hand away and scrambled to her feet. "Of course he'll get better. How can you say he won't? You sound like Susan."

"Eleanor, wait."

She paused.

Doug rose. Took one step toward her, two. "We need to talk. It doesn't have to be like this."

He raised his hand to her face, cupped her cheek. "We

can make it be different this time." And he leaned forward.

Eleanor shoved him back. "What are you doing?"

His wide green eyes roved over her face. "I just thought that we-"

"No! Whatever you thought, you were wrong."

Eleanor grabbed her tray and ran out, but not before she heard him stomp out of the kitchen and slam the back door.

As Eleanor cleared the dishes after breakfast, Susan snapped: "Go roust that old bum you let in. He's either still sleeping or he's already scarpered without paying his bill."

Eleanor focused on her breathing. *It's not her place to give orders, not her home*, she fumed. *In a year I'll be old enough, one more year.* But she said nothing.

She rapped on the old man's door. "Sir? Are you ready to come down for breakfast? I need to clean the room."

No answer. She knocked louder to make sure he could hear her over the roar of the wind outside. "Sir? Are you okay?"

She eased the sliding door open and stepped into the room. The stench of feces turned her stomach.

"Sir?"

Made in the USA
Charleston, SC
03 January 2014